Cinderella must have felt like this....

That thought kept drifting through Lisa's mind. Cinderella. In a four-wheel drive, minus the glass slippers, and not exactly wearing a ball gown. But Cinderella all the same.

Except she didn't believe in fairy tales.

She didn't, did she?

Tad was holding her just right, close but not too close. She was startled to discover that he made her feel rather small and delicate. She had never thought of herself that way. But he was so big, tall and heavily muscled, for all that he moved with such easy grace. Dancing with him—their bodies moving slowly—she could believe this was a man with music in his soul.

She could also believe that she was in trouble. Serious, bone-melting trouble. Trouble like she'd never known in her life.

Too bad she couldn't seem to do anything about it....

Dear Reader,

It's summer. The days are long…hot…just right for romance. And we've got six great romances right here, just waiting for you to settle back and enjoy them. Linda Turner has long been one of your favorite authors. Now, in *I'm Having Your Baby?!* she begins a great new miniseries, THE LONE STAR SOCIAL CLUB. Seems you may rent an apartment in this building single, but you'll be part of a couple before too long. It certainly works that way for Annie and Joe, anyway!

Actually, this is a really great month for miniseries. Ruth Wind continues THE LAST ROUNDUP with *Her Ideal Man,* all about a ranching single dad who's not looking for love but somehow ends up with a pregnant bride. In the next installment of THE WEDDING RING, *Marrying Jake,* Beverly Bird matches a tough cop with a gentle rural woman—and four irresistible kids.

Then there's multi-award-winning Kathleen Creighton's newest, *Never Trust a Lady.* Who would have thought small-town mom Jane Carlysle would end up involved in high-level intrigue—and in love with one very sexy Interpol agent? Maura Seger's back with *Heaven in His Arms,* about how one of life's unluckiest moments—a car crash—somehow got turned into one of life's best, and all because of the gorgeous guy driving the other car. Finally, welcome debut author Raina Lynn. In *A Marriage To Fight For,* she creates a wonderful second-chance story that will leave you hungry for more of this fine new writer's work.

Enjoy them all, and come back next month for more terrific romance—right here in Silhouette Intimate Moments.

Leslie J. Wainger
Senior Editor and Editorial Coordinator

Please address questions and book requests to:
Silhouette Reader Service
U.S.: 3010 Walden Ave., P.O. Box 1325, Buffalo, NY 14269
Canadian: P.O. Box 609, Fort Erie, Ont. L2A 5X3

HEAVEN IN HIS ARMS

MAURA SEGER

Published by Silhouette Books

America's Publisher of Contemporary Romance

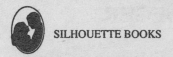 **SILHOUETTE BOOKS**

ISBN 0-373-07803-X

HEAVEN IN HIS ARMS

Books by Maura Seger

Silhouette Intimate Moments

Silver Zephyr #61
Golden Chimera #96
Comes a Stranger #108
Shadows of the Heart #137
Quest of the Eagle #149
Dark of the Moon #162
Happily Ever After #176
Legacy #194
Sea Gate #209
Day and Night #224
Conflict of Interest #236
Unforgettable #253
Change of Plans #280
Painted Lady #342
Caught in the Act #389
Sir Flynn and Lady Constance #404
Castle of Dreams #464
Man of the Hour #492
Prince Conor #520
Full of Surprises #561
The Surrender of Nora #617
Man Without a Memory #675
The Perfect Couple #775
Heaven in His Arms #803

Silhouette Desire

Cajun Summer #282
Treasure Hunt #295
Princess McGee #723

Silhouette Special Edition

A Gift Beyond Price #135

Silhouette Books

Silhouette Christmas Stories 1986
"Starbright"

MAURA SEGER

and her husband, Michael, met while they were both working for the same company. Married after a whirlwind courtship that might have been taken directly from a romance novel, Maura credits her husband's patient support and good humor for helping her fulfill the lifelong dream of being a writer. Currently writing contemporaries for Silhouette and historicals for Harlequin and mainstream, she finds that writing each book is an adventure filled with fascinating people who never fail to surprise her.

Chapter 1

"The severance package is very generous. I really don't think you'll have any problem with it."

Bill Whittiker smiled as he said that. He was on his feet, already ushering her out the door of his office. Lisa thought he looked very satisfied with himself, and why not? She'd been in there a grand total of seven minutes—enough time to be told how much the company appreciated her work, how much they regretted having to "downsize" her, and how soon she had to clear out her desk. There was no doubt about it, Whittiker had this sort of thing down to a science; but then, he'd had plenty of experience.

And she'd had plenty of warning. Well, not plenty. Was there ever plenty of anything in a situation like this? But ever since the Portland, Oregon, advertising agency she worked for had been taken over by a New York City megafirm a month before, the word had been out that a purge was in the making. The new bosses had come in with all the usual assurances about how valued everyone was, no one would be making changes just for the sake of change, they were going to be one big, happy family, and so on and so forth.

Tripe. Pure, unadulterated tripe. Maybe one or two of her fellow employees had been naive—or desperate—enough to believe them, but Lisa had been through this once before and had seen far too many friends go through it in recent years. She'd recognized all the signs. Long before Whittiker asked her to "drop in for a little talk" that day, she'd seen it coming.

Which wasn't to say that it didn't hurt. Hell, she liked her job. Worse yet, she was good at it. And she liked the people she'd been working with, many for the full two years she'd been with the agency. They *had* been like a family, one that was breaking up now.

Her chest felt tight as she walked back to her cubicle. She slumped down in the chair and looked straight ahead. Her desk was cluttered, as usual. Her current assignment was tacked to the drawing board that was a quick swivel of the chair away. There was a small cabinet on wheels to hold art materials, a shelf with reference books, a corkboard festooned with various reminders, a computer, a phone, and that was it. What few personal touches there had been were gone. She really had anticipated being fired. Again.

God, this was the second time in two years. She worked hard, she did a good job, she was utterly reliable and yet here she was, canned again. For just a moment, Lisa let herself really think about how unfair it was. Before she could go too far in that direction, she took a deep breath and sat up straighter. She had to look at the situation honestly. She was single, with no kids, no mortgage, and some actual money in the bank and a few stocks. For the last two years, she'd never bought anything on credit that she couldn't pay for right away. Moreover, even after she'd gotten her current—soon-to-be-former—job, she'd kept up the freelance graphic design and copywriting that had seen her through the stretch between staff positions. That often meant working eighteen hours a day, seven days a week, but besides what it added to her income, it meant she didn't have to feel dependent on any one job ever again. She had a keen appreciation of that now.

There were other people getting the word from Whittiker who were in very different situations than her own. She would save her regrets for them.

She had a week—one week to wrap up what she was doing and get ready to move on with her life. Fine, no problem. But first she was going to have lunch.

In the ladies' room, she glanced at herself in the mirror and grimaced. For someone who was suppos-

edly weathering all this without a flinch, she didn't
look all that good. Her light brown eyes were deeply
shadowed. Her hair—a rich shade of chestnut—tumbled in disarray around her shoulders. She was very
pale; the smattering of freckles across the bridge of
her straight nose stood out starkly. Her mouth looked
unusually full. She had a bad habit of nibbling on her
lower lip when she was nervous.

With a sigh, she set about repairing matters as best
she could. With a firm hand on the brush, she scooped
her hair up to the crown of her head, secured it with
an elastic and fastened it in a loose bun. A few wisps
escaped but the result still seemed more controlled.
She delved into her bag for the few cosmetics she
carried, but lip gloss and a little blush didn't make all
that much of a difference.

Still, she'd done all she could. She smoothed the
knitted top she wore with a wraparound silk skirt that
fell gracefully to her knees. One thing she did tend
to splurge on was pretty clothes, but she'd been careful even about that.

Satisfied she'd done all she could, she left the ladies' room and headed for the elevators. The offices
of New West Advertising were just a couple of blocks
from the restaurant where she was meeting her date
for lunch. She got there a few minutes early, but Brad
was already seated, waiting for her.

He stood when she arrived. She smiled at that, and
at him. Brad Dickerson had wonderful manners. It
was actually one of the first things she'd noticed

about him when they met a month ago. Well, that and
the fact that he was undeniably good-looking. Although only a few inches taller than herself, he had
thick blond hair, attractive features, and a body kept
in shape with daily workouts at the gym. He was always impeccably if conservatively dressed, as befitted
a rising investment analyst.

Brad didn't return her smile, leading Lisa to wonder if she'd left something out of place. She was never
quite as perfectly put together as he was. Her job
didn't require it and her natural inclination was otherwise anyway. But she wondered now if perhaps she
shouldn't have spent just a bit more time with the
hairbrush.

"Hi," she said, a whole lot more brightly than she
felt, and took her seat. He resumed his and nodded.
She thought he was still staring at her rather oddly
but couldn't be sure because a moment later, his expression was masked.

"How are you?" he asked.

It was on the tip of Lisa's tongue to tell him the
truth but she stopped herself. He'd asked just to be
polite, not with any real desire to know. A month ago,
she wouldn't have realized that. But she'd gotten to
know him well enough to recognize when he was just
going through the motions until he could get to what
really interested him.

"Fine," she said, picking up the menu. "And
you?"

"Fine, great. Shall we order?"

They did and for the next few minutes the chitchat was strictly that—meaningless. Lisa found herself wondering why he was doing this. Clearly, he had something on his mind. She wished he would just tell her. The food came and still he seemed determined to say nothing in particular.

They were supposed to go to a concert that weekend. Remembering that suddenly, she mentioned it. "I'm really looking forward to Saturday. Pavarotti's my absolute favorite." Her enthusiasm was warm and unfeigned. She liked most kinds of music but opera was her passion. It might be melodramatic, grandiose, and sometimes just downright silly. She didn't care. Give her an aria and she was happy.

Brad winced. There was no kidding herself about that. She put her fork down and looked right at him. "What's wrong? I thought you were excited about the concert, too."

"I was…. I am…. It's just that…" He took a sip of water and appeared to gird himself. Somberly, he said, "We have to talk."

Lisa didn't move, didn't blink, and for a blessed moment, thought of absolutely nothing. Into that too-brief void, a host of emotions rushed. First, and most strongly, was the sinking realization that she had played this scene before. Those same words, that same tone, the same look. The "We have to talk" scene.

Maybe, just maybe, this time it would be different.

"About what?" she asked, pleased that her voice sounded just a little reedy.

"Us."

Nope, not different. Same scene.

Brad cleared his throat. He looked suitably serious but allowed himself just a shade of anger. "Look, Lisa, this can't come as a big shock to you. We've been dating a month now, seeing each other several times a week, and you still won't..."

She didn't want to hear the rest. Didn't need to. She knew exactly how it would play out.

A month. A whole month. And she still hadn't gone to bed with him. In fact, hadn't permitted him anything more than a few kisses.

"A month isn't all that long to get to know each other," she said quietly. She'd said it before. It hadn't worked then and she would be very surprised if it worked now.

He shook his head, genuinely bewildered. "The thing is, I think you really believe that. First, I thought it was just some kind of game you were playing, and that was okay. I didn't mind going along with it...for a while. But a month's a hell of a long time to invest for nothing."

Lisa took a deep breath. She was getting angry and she didn't like to do that. Anger was bad. It was frightening. But sometimes she just couldn't help it.

"You make it sound like some sort of business deal. Exactly what sort of return on your investment were you looking for?"

The hardness in her voice surprised him. His expression turned cautious. "Hey, there's no reason to get upset. I'm just being honest with you."

They were in a public place. Although that didn't seem to bother Brad any, it did make Lisa feel restrained in what she could say and do—which, all things considered, was just as well.

"Then let me be honest with you, too," she said. "I have too much respect for myself to take intimacy lightly. I won't go into it with someone I barely know."

His mouth twisted in a sneer. "After a month? Hell, what does it take? Two months, six? What exactly do you think you're worth?"

Her chest hurt. For all that she'd been through this before, it wasn't any easier this time. She hated the idea that she had to justify herself, and refused to accept it.

"I'm worth whatever I decide I'm worth," she said quietly. "That's as true for me as it is for anyone else. I won't be pushed or bullied or tricked into doing something I'm not ready for. If you don't understand that, I'm sorry but—"

"No," Brad said. Abruptly, he stood, tossed his napkin onto his unfinished lunch and grabbed his briefcase. "I'm sorry. Sorry I wasted a month with a stuck-up relic from another age." Leaning closer, so that she felt his breath on her cheek, he hissed, "Besides, I'm damn sure you must be frigid."

And with that he was gone. Out the door, out of

her life. Just one more signpost on what seemed more than ever to be the wrong road.

Besides which, he'd stuck her with the check.

Chapter 2

It was done. Tad's fists clenched in satisfaction but outwardly he showed no other sign. He'd been cooped up in the palatial offices of the megacompany that had owned his music imprint for the better part of the day. Worse yet, he'd been forced to tolerate the presence of not only the company executives but a battalion of lawyers—some of them his—accountants, and general hangers-on with no particular function.

His formidable temper was right on the edge, had been for hours, but he'd kept it reined in as sharply as he would have reined a bucking horse. The effort had cost him a pounding headache and a mounting sense of disgust, but he didn't care.

It was done.

He was free.

After fifteen years in the music business, the last seven of them as a superstar, he was free. He'd severed his ties to the company that had virtually owned him in the beginning, then tried to ruthlessly exploit him and when that had failed, done everything possible to manipulate and control him. He hadn't allowed that. Using the immense power his string of platinum hits guaranteed, he'd made the music-company executives dance to his own tune. In the process, he'd acquired a full measure of satisfaction and an immense personal fortune.

But now it was over and he couldn't feel anything but relief. He was walking away from a life many people would have killed for, and he was glad of it. He was thirty-six years old and he didn't sleep under his own roof more than twenty nights a year. He had his pick of women but knew full well that they wanted the star, not the man. He had a daughter he didn't know and a place he thought could be home if he ever let it.

He stood, unfolding his full six-foot-three-inch length with fluid grace. The charcoal-gray suit he wore lay smoothly over his massive shoulders and broad chest. He had not taken his jacket off, only opened it over the finely woven white linen shirt and striped silk tie. He fastened it again now, a silent male signal that the meeting was over.

He was leaving.

Jason Roberts jumped up. The music-company

CEO was a good half-foot shorter than Tad and thirty pounds heavier. Sweat beaded on his forehead. He put out both well-manicured hands beseechingly.

"Tad, please, don't do this. It's still not too late. We can work things out. Just tell us what you want."

Although he was tempted to laugh, Tad stopped himself. After all this time, all the words that had been said, Roberts still persisted in believing it was some kind of negotiating ploy. He just couldn't wrap his greedy little head around the fact that Tad was really finished.

"There's nothing to work out," Tad said as he stepped around the executive and headed for the door. "I've got what I came for and now I'm going home."

Nobody else moved. So far as he knew, nobody even blinked. They just sat there in stunned silence, his own people included, and watched him walk away.

On the table behind him, untouched, were the papers documenting an offer of one hundred million dollars needing only his signature to make real.

A signature he would never give.

Limos were waiting in the garage for the phalanx of lawyers and the rest, but he'd had the foresight to come in his own car. It was a sweet little Italian number, low-slung, black, and powerful enough to be interesting. He'd only had it a couple of weeks, and his life didn't exactly leave him much opportunity to enjoy it. That was going to change, starting right now.

The clock above the garage security booth read five

o'clock exactly when Tad purred up the ramp and angled the car smoothly into traffic.

Lisa had gone back to the office after lunch. She had no good reason for doing so, just habit. Sitting in her cubicle, she stared at the opposite wall and tried to make some sense out of the sudden shambles all around her.

So far today, she'd lost her job and her boyfriend. Her lips pressed together tightly. She absolutely, positively was not going to cry. Why should she? If nothing else, things were bound to get better.

Hell, they would just about have to.

Despite the growing desire to rush home, crawl into bed, pull the covers up over her head and sob her heart out, she forced herself to stay right where she was until five o'clock. She didn't actually get any work done—that would have been asking too much. But she did manage just enough of a semblance of normality to salvage her pride.

At 5:02 p.m. she got into the elevator. At 5:05 p.m. she crossed the street to the parking lot and retrieved her battered four-wheel-drive vehicle, the same one she'd had since college. It might not look like much, but it got her where she was going. And it was fully paid for. At 5:08 p.m., she paid the attendant, wished him a good-evening and headed into traffic.

Tad propped an elbow on the rolled-down window, rested the other lightly on the wheel, and changed lanes—again. Traffic was fairly heavy—he supposed it was rush hour but didn't think much about that. He wasn't in any particular hurry but the pleasure he felt now that the meeting was over sent a surge of energy through him. The powerful sports car responded to the slightest pressure. He slipped in front of a taxi, caught a yellow light just before it turned red, and hugged a corner.

His hotel was under a mile away. He could have chosen one closer to the meeting site, but he liked the sedate anonymity of the place that catered to travelers for whom the word *budget* had no actual meaning.

All the same, he was thinking about checking out, instead of spending a second night as he'd originally planned. If he drove straight through, he would be home by dawn. The idea had definite appeal. He was still considering it when he turned another corner. The light up ahead had just gone red. Tad failed to notice. It never occurred to him that it was years since he'd done much driving for himself, or that the lack of regular practice could make a difference. Nor did he take into account that the meeting had left him tired and distracted, for all that he was well-pleased.

His mind on other things, he went straight through the red light.

And straight into another vehicle.

Well, not exactly straight. He hit her more to the side right in the front on the passenger side. The crash of crunching metal and breaking glass drowned out the usual city sounds. Hard on it came silence. Traffic stopped, pedestrians halted, and everyone took a good—if resigned—look to see what had happened.

Tad sat shock-still behind the wheel for a moment. He realized immediately that it was his fault. The hood of his car had popped up, preventing him from seeing what he'd hit. Steam poured from the engine. He had to get out…do something….

He flipped the handle to open the door. For a moment, nothing happened. He had to bring real strength to bear before the door finally yielded and then, only grudgingly.

By the time he got out of the car, he could hear sirens off in the distance. A few passersby lingered to watch but most went on their way. The other drivers were making their way around the accident scene, slowing traffic but not stopping it.

He came around to the other side of the hood and got his first glimpse of what he'd hit. A four-wheel drive that looked as though it had seen better days even before he plowed into it. The impact had left a new and sizable dent in the right front but he couldn't see any other damage. At least not to the vehicle.

His eyes searched for the driver. No one was behind the wheel but a young woman was standing near the car, looking it over. From her frown, he gathered she had more than a passing interest.

With relief, he saw that she seemed to be uninjured. It took a moment more for him to note that she was extremely attractive. Slightly above average height for a woman and slender, she had chestnut hair scooped up loosely at the crown of her head, and delicate features. She was wearing a knitted top tucked into a wraparound skirt that left enough of her slim, shapely legs bare to definitely grab his attention.

Until he realized it and shook his head ruefully. He'd just been involved in his first ever automobile accident and all he could think about was a woman's legs? The stress of the last few months must be getting to him more than he'd realized.

She noticed him then and her frown deepened. He stepped forward quickly. "I'm really sorry. This was my fault and of course, I'll take full responsibility."

Her eyes were a golden shade of brown. They looked at him for what seemed like a long moment before she said, "You ran a red light."

"Yes, I did. I'm sorry."

The second apology seemed to get through to her where the first had not. She sighed and to his surprise, shrugged. "These things happen." After a second, she added, "You are insured, aren't you?"

"Certainly." Of course he was. His personal staff would never have allowed a lapse like that.

She nodded. "Okay. Then I suppose we should get the formalities out of the way."

He agreed and went back to his car to find the registration and so on. She was copying down the numbers he gave her when the police car arrived.

The officer was young, in his early twenties, and acutely professional. He surveyed the scene, observed each of them, and relaxed slightly. Tad didn't have to wonder why. Nobody was hurt, there was no fight, it was all just routine.

Or it was until the officer looked at him again and did a double take.

"Hey," he said, grinning, "you're Tad Jenkins."

The young woman—she'd said her name was Lisa Preston—glanced from the cop to him and back again. She looked puzzled.

The cop's smile broadened. "I'll be damned. You really are, aren't you?"

Tad stifled a groan. He ought to be used to this. But the reality was that it had been years since he'd gone out in public alone without any entourage or guards of any kind unless he'd first made a real effort to disguise his appearance. He had a formidable collection of headgear and sunglasses for just that purpose. The problem was that he didn't have any of it right then.

Several people who were standing off to the side heard what the cop had said.

"Thought so," one commented to nobody in particular.

"Tad Jenkins, how about that?"

"Right here? What happened?"

"Ran into somebody...straight through a red light."

There was a little good-natured laughter but mostly people just stared. They would be taking in every detail, getting ready to repeat it all first chance they got.

He couldn't really blame them, although he didn't

understand it, either. He'd never understood what the big deal was about seeing a celebrity. Maybe it was just that it gave people something to talk about.

Several more people, just arriving on the scene, heard what was being said and stopped to watch. The crowd began to grow.

Meanwhile, the cop had remembered himself enough to whip out his book, do a quick write-up of the accident and hand Tad a citation.

"Sorry about that, Mr. Jenkins," he murmured, "but you did say you ran the red light."

"Yeah, I did." Tad pocketed the summons while keeping an eye on the crowd. It was growing faster. He kept hearing his name being mentioned. Several people were pointing, and edging a little closer.

"If we're done..." he said.

The cop looked a little reluctant but he wasn't going to push it. "I guess so.... Miss Preston...?"

"Seems fine with me," she replied. It was then that Tad noticed something odd. She was looking at him, all right, the same as everyone else, yet not the same. Whereas there was recognition in their eyes, hers held only puzzlement.

"I assume you'll call your insurance company, Mr. Jenkins?" She said his name slowly, as though thinking she ought to know it. But didn't.

"Sure..." He spoke absently, focused on the pleasant novelty of meeting someone who didn't know who he was. Better yet, meeting an extremely attractive young woman who didn't know.

Too bad it hadn't happened under different circumstances. The cop was done. They were free to go. Or at least, she was. Judging by the state of his car, he wasn't going anywhere. Unless he wanted to do it on foot, which meant first he would have to make his way through the crowd.

The large and getting-larger crowd.

He made a split-second decision. Lisa Preston was buckling her seat belt when he came up beside her. He gave her his best stage smile, the one that made women from sixteen to infinity act like deranged groupies, and said, "I hate to ask this, but could you possibly give me a lift?"

She looked at him, looked at what was left of his car, then looked at the crowd. He thought she was about to refuse. But she surprised him.

Hesitantly, obviously uncertain about what she was doing, she said, "Hop in."

Chapter 3

She'd really done it now. Let a strange man into her car with hardly a second thought. Really smart. Except he wasn't supposed to be a stranger, not exactly. She'd picked up on that clearly enough. Everyone else seemed to know who he was. The problem was that she didn't. She had the vague feeling that she ought to, but that didn't help any.

Nor did the way he looked. Sweet heaven, the man was gorgeous. From the bottom of his high-gloss boots—unusual with the elegant business suit but undeniably masculine—to the top of his sleek black hair fastened in a queue at the nape of his neck, he was easily the most compelling man she had ever seen. His eyes were dark beneath slanting brows, his nose firm, his mouth hard. He looked as though he'd been carved from stone caressed by sun. The thought, so unlikely for her, sent a shiver down her spine. She tightened her hands on the wheel and stared straight ahead.

"Where to?" she asked. The sooner she got him where he was going, the better. The only contact they would be having after that would be through the insurance company, and *that* suited her just fine.

He mentioned a hotel she'd noticed once or twice in passing but had never been in. "If that won't take you out of your way," he added courteously.

"No, that's fine." She should have stopped right then. There was no reason to engage him in conversation. What could they talk about, after all? *Have you caused many traffic accidents? Was that the first car you've wrecked? Where exactly did you learn to drive?*

"I take it you're from out of town?" The words popped out before she could stop them. Lisa glanced at him. He was looking at her curiously.

"Yes, I am. I was here for a business meeting."

He paused, as though expecting her to say something more. When she didn't, he continued looking at her. She knew he was doing that despite her having locked her eyes on the road again. She could feel it, as though his gaze actually touched her.

It was an extremely disconcerting sensation. She breathed a sigh of relief when she saw the hotel up ahead.

"We're here." Rather more quickly than she

would have under normal circumstances, she angled the vehicle into the open space in front of the entrance. Instantly, two ornately uniformed doormen appeared and began waving her off irately. Or at least they did until they caught sight of Tad sitting beside her. Then they were all smiles.

Both doors were opened. "Sorry, Mr. Jenkins," one of the men said. "We didn't realize it was you."

The other, the one on Lisa's side, said, "Just leave the keys, miss. I'll take care of it."

"That isn't necessary." She was about to explain that she wasn't staying when Tad came around to her side of the car. He looked down at her from far too great a height. His eyes were very intent. He wasn't smiling. His hand—big, sinewy, hard—reached out to her.

Softly, as though determined not to alarm her, he said, "The least I can do is offer you dinner."

She was crazy. There was no other possible explanation for what she'd done. Letting him in the car hadn't been bad enough. She'd had to agree to have dinner with him?

Maybe she'd bumped her head in the accident and hadn't realized it. That could account for her extraordinary behavior. Certainly, it had nothing to do with the fact that a single look from Tad Jenkins—whoever he might be—made her feel weak, trembling and hot inside.

Flu! That was it, she was coming down with the

flu. It had been going around the office the last few weeks and now it was her turn. She smiled to herself. What a relief. She would be sick as a dog for a few days, then she would be fine. It had nothing to do with Tad Jenkins at all.

Right. He had paused briefly to speak with a man she guessed was the concierge. When he returned his attention to her, her stomach did a long, slow flip-flop.

He smiled, which she decided right then he really shouldn't be allowed to do, and took her arm lightly at the elbow. "All set. We'll have dinner here, if you don't mind."

Lisa glanced around the lobby. She didn't see anything that indicated a restaurant. In fact, nothing she saw looked much like a hotel lobby at all. There was no reception desk, no banks of phones, no escalators, no crisply pleasant employees in matching blazers, no people coming and going. Instead, they seemed to be standing in the grand hall of a palatial private residence. Two stories above them, the ceiling was festooned with chubby cherubs and rotund goddesses who appeared to have misplaced their clothes. Ornately carved columns spanned the distance to the gleaming marble floor partially covered by Persian rugs. Several discrete sitting areas were furnished with what even her uninformed eye could recognize as antiques. Similarly, the paintings in gilded frames were undoubtedly originals, and looked as though they had previously graced an English country estate.

The effect was so blatantly privileged and so incongruous with the workaday world she inhabited that she was unsure what to make of it all. She'd never known such places existed, much less what went on in them.

Which brought her to a rather more important point. He'd said they were dining there. Since she saw no sign of a restaurant, how exactly did he plan to manage that?

Her back stiffened. If he thought for one moment that she was going to have dinner with him in his room—no, not room, it would be a suite—he could *hasta la vista* himself out of her way, pronto.

Frowning, she turned to him, fully prepared to clear up that little matter right then and there, only to find that he was grinning. It wasn't the smile she'd seen before—the devastating, well-practiced, melt-the-knees smile. It was a wholehearted, unabashed grin. And it was just a little bit chiding.

"They have private dining rooms here," he said. For good measure, he added, "Although private's a little misleading. The service is excellent—constant attention, waiters back and forth all the time, you know."

She didn't, having never experienced any such thing. But she could imagine and that reassured her. Actually, the reassurance came from his bothering to explain in the first place. He could have ignored her concern, or belittled it. Belatedly, she realized that she was surprised he hadn't.

They were shown to a large, opulently furnished dining room a short distance from the entry hall. One entire wall was taken up by floor-to-ceiling windows, the heavy curtains drawn across them. A fireplace stood opposite, wood crackling softly beneath a marble mantel. A comfortable seating area was arranged in front of the fire. The oval dining table was nearby. It could seat eight but the extra place settings were being removed, leaving only two.

The concierge hovered, exchanging a few more quiet words with Tad. Then they were alone, but only briefly. As he had said, waiters arrived at once, drawing out chairs, proffering menus, filling crystal water goblets, lighting the slim white tapers in the silver candelabras that braced either end of the table.

Music played softly in the background. The air carried the perfume of roses and lilies artfully arranged on the sideboards.

It was all rather magical.

A sense of bemusement crept over Lisa. What had seemed like the worst day of her life had suddenly turned into something altogether different.

Far in the back of her mind, a little voice whispered: *Oh, yeah?*

He studied her across the table, watching the way the candlelight played over her face. It had come to him in the past few minutes that she didn't know she was beautiful. He couldn't quite figure out how that could be, but he was sure it was, all the same.

She wasn't wearing any mascara. He'd looked closely enough to be sure of that. But her lashes were so thick and curling that adding anything to them would have been a sacrilege. She wasn't wearing any other makeup either. Her skin glowed with health. A smattering of freckles marched across her nose. Her lips were full, rose-hued and very, very tempting.

The intensity of his response to her surprised him. He'd had—how many?—beautiful women. It didn't particularly please him that he couldn't have even guessed the number. In his younger, oat-sowing days, he'd taken everything fame flung his way and not questioned it. That had changed; *he'd changed.* But he still wasn't above noticing beauty, especially not when it came backlit by warmth and spontaneity.

She was laughing at something the waiter had said. Tad caught himself glaring at the man who fortunately didn't notice. But then, how could he when he was so busy fawning over Lisa?

"That will be all," Tad said. He knew his tone was abrupt, even autocratic. He just didn't care. He wanted to be alone with her, if only for the few minutes before the first course was served.

She sat back, laughter still playing at the corners of her mouth, and studied him as unabashedly as he had studied her.

"I have the feeling I should recognize you."

He shrugged, feeling unaccountably self-conscious. Carefully, he said, "I used to be in the music business." *Used to be.* He liked the sound of that.

"What kind of music?"

"Country and western, mostly." It would happen now. She would realize who he was. He felt a stab of regret at that.

Instead, she just nodded with no sign of recognition at all. "That explains it."

"Explains what?"

Almost apologetically, as though she didn't want to hurt his feelings, she said, "I'm an opera buff."

The wine steward proffered a bottle for his inspection. Tad went through the tasting ritual while his attention remained completely on her.

"Opera?"

"Domingo, Pavarotti, Carreras, you know?"

"Oh, yeah, sure."

He'd caught part of an opera once...on public television. A fat woman in a blond wig with braids had been marching back and forth across a stage shrieking something about Valhalla.

"You like that stuff?"

She took a sip of the wine and nodded. "Hmm, ever since I was a kid. My brothers would beg for tickets to a baseball game or the circus. I was thrilled to sit in the last row at *Aida*."

"Do you like any other kind of music?"

"Some classical and I adore Copland. His *Appalachian Spring* may be the greatest piece of American music ever written."

Tad relaxed slightly. He knew nothing about opera and was happy to keep it that way. But Copland was another matter. "His *Fanfare for the Common Man* is better."

Her eyebrows rose slightly. "You really think so?"

"It's more...muscular."

"Yes, I suppose it is, if that's what you like, but I still think..."

They were off and running. She really did know music, at least, her kind. But so did he. It had, after all, been his life. They swapped opinions, often disagreeing, enjoying it when they found common ground. She admitted her ignorance in vast areas; he did the same for his. But he held firm on the subject of opera.

"I just don't get it," he said. "The shrieking and bellowing, the ridiculous costumes, the—"

"Shrieking? Bellowing? How can you say that? Think of the incredible voice control it takes, think of the artistry, the pageantry, the—"

He held up his hands, laughing. "Okay, maybe I should give it another chance someday." Maybe he would if she was there to help him through it. But he didn't say that, instinct telling him not to pressure her. She was relaxed now, enjoying herself. Her guard was down and he meant to keep it that way.

Dinner had come and gone. He supposed it had been excellent, as usual, but he couldn't have actually described anything they'd eaten. The waiters were unobtrusively attentive, bringing and removing plates, refilling wineglasses.

And still the music played.

Her eyes looked like gold emerging from darkness. He had never seen anything quite like them. Never been with a woman who made him feel so simply himself. Never felt...

He stood, so swiftly that he surprised both of them. Again, as he had earlier, he held out his hand to her. And again, he smiled.

"Would you care to dance?"

Cinderella must have felt like this. That thought kept drifting through Lisa's mind, rolling slowly over and over. Cinderella. In a four-wheel drive, minus the glass slippers, and not exactly wearing a ballgown. But Cinderella all the same.

Too bad she didn't believe in fairy tales.

She didn't, did she?

He was holding her just right, close but not too close. One hand held hers, their fingers interlaced. The other hand was warm and strong against her back.

She was startled to discover that he made her feel rather small and delicate. She had never thought of herself that way. But he was so unusually big, tall and heavily muscled, for all that he moved with such easy grace.

Dancing with him—their bodies moving slowly— she could believe this was a man with music in his soul.

She could also believe that she was in trouble. Serious trouble.

Too bad she couldn't seem to do anything about it.

* * *

He shouldn't have asked her to dance. Touching her was more than he'd bargained for. She felt so right, slender yet strong, feminine in a way he couldn't really grasp but sensed was somehow crucially different from the hard-edged women he had known.

She smelled like heather.

God, where had that thought come from? He'd only been to Scotland once, on a concert tour, and he sure as hell hadn't spent his time sniffing the heather. But he had caught a whiff of it, just once, and apparently it had lodged somewhere deep down in his brain.

Until Lisa brought it right back up.

Speaking of up—

He didn't know whether to be amused or chagrined. Just holding her, swaying gently to the music, had him intensely aroused. If he moved even the smallest distance closer to her, she was going to be aware of it.

And then—

What would her response be? Satisfaction? Anticipation? Or would she be nervous and concerned? He couldn't remember ever having to wonder before, and he wasn't sure what to do about that. Instinct warned him that this woman was different. She was too gentle, too natural. She required special handling.

The waiters had finished clearing the table, except for the wine, and had gone. They were alone with the music, the fire, and each other.

His hand moved at the small of her back. He stroked her slowly, gentling her, accustoming her to his touch. His head bent, his breath brushing the curve of her cheek in the instant before his mouth took hers.

Trouble. Serious, bone-melting trouble. Trouble like she'd never known before in her life.

But, sweet heaven, it felt so good.

His lips were firm, warm, seeking. Hers parted on a sigh. His tongue slipped in slowly, coaxing rather than demanding. When she offered no resistance, he deepened the kiss.

His arms tightened around her. They were no longer dancing but the music seemed to be inside her, soaring, blocking out all thought.

It was just a kiss. She'd been kissed plenty and had never made a fool of herself over it.

Of course, she hadn't actually been kissed like this and she was still just enough in control to realize it.

Trouble.

Tad Jenkins—whatever he "used to be" in the music business—was big trouble right there, that second, in the opulent private dining room with the music playing and her brain merrily shutting down, figuring it wouldn't be needed for a while.

Wrong. Very wrong. She needed all systems on go, firing on all cylinders, all the little logic boards running full tilt. She needed cold, clear thinking and she needed it right now.

Too bad she was melting.

His mouth moved, nuzzling behind her ear, caressing her throat, finding its way to the ultrasensitive skin between her collarbones.

She moaned. The sound just slipped out. She couldn't help it anymore than she could help the fact that the hands that should have been pushing him away were instead drawing him closer.

He raised his head, his eyes meeting hers. He looked...surprised, even uncertain. Or perhaps she imagined it, for the look was gone in an instant. His mouth locked on hers, hard and insistent.

At the same time, he backed her toward the couch in front of the fireplace. She was stretched out on it, her legs entwined with his, before she even realized what was happening.

The palms of his hands were callused. She could feel their roughness through the thin silk of her skirt as they moved up her thighs and above her waist, to cup her breasts.

A tremor shook her. She had never felt like this, never responded with such instant, helpless yearning. Yearning so great that it smothered over the very natural sense of danger that should have been taking control at that point.

He murmured hoarsely, the words indistinguishable but the sound alone enough to make the muscles of her abdomen clench. His hands slipped beneath her knitted top, easing it up to reveal her breasts not at all concealed by the sheer lace of her bra.

"Beautiful," he whispered and this time she heard

him, just as his fingers snapped open the front closure of the bra, baring her completely to his gaze.

And to his mouth. Her nipples were already hard, drawn like tight little rosebuds. His tongue licked them over and over—long, slow strokes followed by quick, swirling tastes. Her back arched, her hands sliding into his hair to hold him more firmly.

Just when she thought she couldn't bear it any longer, he took a nipple fully into his mouth, sucking her vigorously. The sensation pierced her throughout. She cried softly, her legs opening as though of their own accord.

He felt that and did not hesitate. The day was warm enough that she hadn't worn stockings. There was only the thin covering of her panties beneath the silk skirt. He stroked her through it, again and again, as he continued to suckle first one breast, then the other.

"It's all right," he murmured, his voice thick. "I'll make this perfect for you. Open for me, baby." His fingers slid beneath the fabric, finding her delicate flesh, reaching into—

A jolt of pure panic roared through Lisa. With hideous suddenness, reality intruded. She was lying on a couch, spread wide, her breasts bared, being touched intimately by a man she hadn't even met scant hours before.

The horror that filled her was only slightly softened by the knowledge that she had wanted this as much as he did.

That hadn't changed. But what had was the recollection of herself, of who she was as a woman and a person. The self she was about to irrevocably betray.

"Stop," she said and pushed hard against his shoulders at the same time she tried to wiggle out from underneath him.

He didn't seem to hear her, his fingers continuing to stroke, his mouth at her nipple, his tongue—

"Stop!" Her efforts became frantic. She was determined to get away.

Slowly, that penetrated the fog of passion that robbed Tad of reason. He didn't understand what had happened or why. But he sat up all the same, staring at her.

"What's wrong?"

She looked at him as though he was mad. "Wrong? You have to ask that? You can't... You had no right...."

Understanding dawned. His scowl was dark and savage. "If you're thinking of crying rape, baby, forget it. Nobody's going to hear you."

Real fear came then, driving out Lisa's outrage. The waiters were long gone. She had no idea if there was anyone even left in this part of the hotel. Nor did she have any idea of how far the staff would go to serve and protect a valued guest.

"Besides," he continued as his weight left her abruptly, "my lawyers will need all of about fifteen seconds to shred you."

"Lawyers?"

He was walking away, putting distance between

them. She was relieved, but confused. Cool air touched her breasts. Her cheeks flushed as she drew her clothes back into place and stood.

"I came here for dinner," she reminded him. "That was it."

He turned, his expression so threatening that it was all she could do not to take a step backward. But that would have tumbled her onto the couch again—something she definitely didn't want to do.

"You led me to believe otherwise."

She had. That was the truly horrible part about it. She had completely succumbed to his first kiss, done nothing to resist, responded with more heat and passion than she had ever known, and not objected in any way until they were on the very brink.

A feeling of very real shame swept her. She couldn't blame him for this when she herself had been a full participant.

"I'm sorry," she said quietly. "I realize my attitudes are different from those of most people. I shouldn't have led you to expect anything other than..."

She never got to finish. The look he gave her was pure scorn. His gaze swept her up and down scathingly. "Thanks for the ride," he said. "So long."

She was well and truly dismissed, and she knew it. Her face flaming, she picked up her bag and got out of that room as quickly as she could.

Chapter 4

Four days after what she'd come to think of—with uncharacteristic sarcasm—as her "perfect day," Lisa finished cleaning out her desk, took one last look around her cubicle, and walked out toward the elevators for the last time.

She paused along the way to say goodbye to several friends, most of whom were also leaving. The purge had been brutal. More than half the staff had been fired, their work transferred to the "lucky" ones who would be staying.

Lisa had no doubts where that would lead. The agency hadn't been overstaffed to begin with. Everyone had really worked, but in an atmosphere that allowed for relaxed exchanges of information, camaraderie and creativity. That was over now. She honestly couldn't envy those who had kept their jobs, and wondered how long very many of them would last.

Downstairs, she put the carton with her belongings into her car and slid behind the wheel. She was planning to take a few days off to get herself organized and decide what to do. Or maybe it was just to absorb the shock of everything that had happened to her.

In a handful of days, she had lost her job and her boyfriend, and come incredibly close to losing her self-respect with a man she didn't even know. Of the three, it was the last that haunted her.

Try though she did—and she tried desperately— she couldn't get Tad out of her mind. He seemed to be there every time she turned around, her thoughts constantly on him.

And at night, when she tried to sleep, it was even worse. Then her body was free to remind her of exactly how much she had wanted him. How full a participant she had been in what had happened—and almost happened—between them.

It was torture, plain and simple. Because of it, she'd given no thought at all to Brad. He might as well have never existed. She couldn't even focus on the fact that she was no longer employed, although that would have to change soon.

She hated the idea of raiding her savings to pay the bills but she would have to if she didn't get moving quickly. The great severance package Whittiker had ballyhooed amounted to a grand total of two weeks' pay. She had money coming in from several freelance assignments she'd completed in the last month or so. But that wouldn't last long, either.

She needed to either get a new job or get serious about new freelance assignments. Either way, she couldn't waste any more time thinking about a man she was never going to see again.

She'd actually gone so far as to make a visit to a music store where she quickly discovered who Tad Jenkins actually was. The guy behind the counter had laughed at her ignorance. She couldn't blame him. If she'd been paying any attention at all to popular culture in the last few years, she would have known perfectly well who he was. Hell, she might have owned several of his albums.

The temptation to buy one had been awful. Only her instinct for self-preservation stopped her. She absolutely could not sit alone in her apartment listening to his voice and tormenting herself. No way.

For three days after that, she'd walked past the music store but hadn't gone in. Then her job was over and she had no reason to be on that street anyway.

Not that there weren't plenty of other music stores. She was just going to have to stay out of them until this—whatever this was—was over.

She would concentrate on work. She would devote herself to it. She would become so completely absorbed in slogans, jingles, snappy ad copy and riveting layouts that she would have no time or energy to think of anything else.

Right.

She found a parking spot right in front of her apartment building and slipped into it before anyone could beat her to it. Stopping to get her mail, she saw that two of the checks she'd been expecting had arrived. The elevator door was standing open. She got in, lugging her carton, and pushed the button for her floor.

Maybe her luck was starting to change...just a little.

Inside her apartment, she set the carton down, flipped on the air-conditioning and took a bottle of mineral water from the refrigerator. She would grab a shower, change her clothes, and get started on the rest of her life.

Half an hour later, turning off the water and reaching for a towel, she heard the phone ring. She got to it just before the answering machine would have picked up.

With just a little more luck, this would be the freelance agency she used. Anticipating that, she said, "Hello?"

There was silence for an instant, then a too-well-remembered voice replied, "Lisa? It's Tad...Tad Jenkins. I called to—"

Her hand had a viselike grip on the receiver. Her stomach flip-flopped. Before she could think, she said, "This number is unlisted. How did you get it?"

"It took some doing but—"

"You shouldn't have. I really don't want to speak with you."

Silence again. She had to hang up. She was crazy not to have done so already. But the man's voice alone was enough to make her go weak at the knees. That and all the memories it provoked.

"I can understand that, but I—"

"Look, what happened was really out of character for me. I'd just had a really bad day...lost my job, broke up with my boyfriend, car accident, all at once. Otherwise, I would never..." She broke off. Never have what? Never have felt such passion? Never have come so close to betraying herself?

"Never have acted like some dumb little groupie."

She heard a quick in-drawing of breath and then his voice, very low and hard: "Is that what you were doing?"

Lisa gulped. She was suddenly very close to tears and she couldn't bear that he would know. On a thread of sound, she murmured, "Goodbye, Tad."

The receiver settled back into the phone. She stared at it for several moments, her hand pressed to her mouth. Deep within her was a twisting sense of sorrow she could neither understand nor deny.

Dismally, she told herself she had done the right thing. Yes, she'd been rude and abrupt, but she'd had to be in order to protect herself. But for all that, she couldn't help but wonder why he had even bothered to call.

Hours later, lying in bed and trying vainly to sleep, she realized she had never given him a chance to say.

* * *

He had to be nuts. There was no other possible explanation. Why else would he still be thinking about a rude, insufferable, cold little tease?

Why would he be remembering how her lips felt like warm velvet beneath his own, how her body moved with feminine grace, how her hair held the scent of heather?

Why would he be torturing himself like this?

He was supposed to be savoring his liberation from a career that for all its success had become a prison. He was supposed to be relaxing and enjoying his long-neglected home. He was supposed to be getting on with the rest of his life.

Right.

Instead, all he seemed able to do was think of a woman with eyes torn from the sun and a mouth made for dreams.

With a low groan, he turned over in the huge bed and willed himself to sleep. Without success. Long after the moon sank low in the night sky and even the owls in the stables beyond the house sought their rest, Tad continued to lie awake.

His heavily muscled arms were folded behind his head. His long, hard body stretched out beneath the finely woven linen sheet. His eyes, gleaming there in the darkness, were thoughtful.

The first gray light of dawn was just touching the horizon when he smiled.

Chapter 5

"Great news," Mary Chamers said. The plump, middle-aged woman gave Lisa a big grin and gestured toward the chair facing her desk.

"Have I got a job for you. You're going to love this." She shuffled through a stack of files, extracted one and waved it in the air. "I said to myself, Lisa's due for a change of luck. That's what I said and wouldn't you know it—poof—it happened." Her grin widened. "I feel like a fairy godmother."

Lisa shook her head, laughing, as she sat down. She'd known Mary Chamers for three years, liked and respected the woman who for all her pleasant manner was an extremely hardheaded and successful agent. But Lisa had never seen her so enthused.

"This doesn't have anything to do with announcing

the Second Coming, does it?'' she asked, matching Mary's grin.

''Don't joke. Were talking about a little slice of paradise on earth. Ever hear of a place called Teal River?''

Lisa had but it took her a moment to place it. ''About five hundred miles east of here in the foothills of the Rockies?''

''That's it. Seems like someone's been buying up land all along the Teal River for years now, put together about fifty thousand acres. The plan is to keep most of it as a nature preserve but selectively develop a few parcels for a very upscale resort and community—'' she picked up the file and read a passage from it ''—in harmony with and dedicated to the protection of the natural world.''

''Sounds great,'' Lisa agreed. ''If it's for real. Is it, or is that just the sales pitch?''

''It's for real,'' Mary said emphatically. ''The outfit spearheading this already has a stellar record for environmental protection in the development of resorts all around the world. This is intended to be the flagship operation, the best of the best. There'll be a full-court press for the promotion rollout—print, TV, you name it.'' She put down the folder and looked right at Lisa. ''And they want you to write all the copy.''

She sat back, a supremely pleased look on her face. ''How about them apples?''

''Some apples...'' Lisa murmured slowly. She was

having a little trouble taking it all in. The assignment sounded like the dream job to end all dream jobs. She would be handling a project she could actually believe in, backed up by an organization that really sounded like it knew what it was doing.

So why did she have the niggling feeling there was a catch?

"Why me? Why not just go to a major agency? Face it, Mary, freelancers don't usually get assignments like this."

"True enough, but it seems the job you did for the Bahamian Tourist Council last year caught their eye. So did the spread for Club Carib's new operation. They think you've got the right touch. If you were still on staff they would have gone to the agency. Since you aren't..." She spread her hands and shrugged.

Since she wasn't, she could still have the job as a freelancer. She wouldn't be accountable to anyone other than the Teal River honchos. There wouldn't be any agency middlemen to muck things up.

Better and better.

"You're right," Lisa said finally. "This really is an incredible break. I'd have to be crazy to turn it down."

Mary laughed. She gave Lisa a chiding look. "Care to hear about the money before you commit?"

"Oh, sure, the money... I did mean to—"

"It's okay, sweetheart. That's what you've got

Aunt Mary for." She named a figure that made Lisa's mouth drop open.

"You can't be serious."

"Of course I can. I told them they'd be getting a bargain, but maybe you'd take it because you really cared about the environment."

"You didn't. You know that's more money than I've ever made."

"I know it, you know it. They don't know it. And that suits me just fine. You're damn good and you really do happen to be the perfect person for this job. I just wish I could go to Teal River with you."

Right about then it began to dawn on Lisa that this was for real. She was going to be paid an exorbitant amount of money to do what she liked best for a place that sounded like heaven on earth. When her luck changed, it *really* changed.

An hour later, she was out on the sidewalk, thinking about what she had to do next. She would have to get packed for a stay of at least several weeks and that included not only clothes but her notebook computer, materials for sketching layouts, and anything else she could conceivably need. Mary had warned her that Teal River was pretty remote. Until the new road was put in and the community actually got up and running, the nearest "civilization" was a good couple of hundred miles away.

The idea of being so isolated didn't faze her. She'd lived in cities most of her life, but she didn't particularly like them. The country suited her far better. She

was delighted to finally get a chance to spend some
time in it.

Two days later, having arranged for her mail to be
forwarded, notified the building superintendent that
she was going to be away, farmed out her plants to
neighbors, and loaded up her car, she was on her way.

She was briefly tempted to drive straight through
but the idea of arriving at her new job road-weary
didn't appeal. Instead, she overnighted along the way
at a cookie-cutter motel with the regulation clean
rooms, ice machines and pool.

The next morning, she was up early, grabbed a
quick breakfast, and got back on the road. She hadn't
gone far before the view out the windshield began to
change. Whereas before, one small town had rolled
into another, complete with interchangeable shopping
strips and fast-food places, suddenly the signs of human habitation became scarcer.

She drove for several miles without passing a single building and when she finally did, it was no more
than a small gas station. She stopped there to top off
her tank and check her directions. She lingered to
enjoy the view.

For the past hour or so, she'd been aware of the
car climbing as the road slanted upward. It was no-
ticeable enough to even slightly alter the pressure in
her ears. The air was cooler, making her glad she'd
packed the clothes she had. It also smelled incredibly
fresh. She breathed in deeply and smiled.

Ahead of her, the land rose first in softly rolling

hills but changing quickly to small mountains. Far off, in the distance, she could see the blue-gray mist concealing the proud steeples of the Rockies themselves. Even at this time of year, there would be snow along many of the peaks. She shivered slightly and with some reluctance, got back into the car. She would have liked to stand there longer, just drinking it all in with her eyes. But there would be time for that later.

Anxious now to reach her destination, she drove on without another stop until she came to the rutted dirt road with the hand-lettered wooden sign that read simply: Teal River Preserve.

Turning onto the road, Lisa slipped the vehicle into four-wheel drive and went slowly. She knew from the plans she'd studied that eventually this road would be widened and paved. But that was a while off yet and in the meantime it called for caution.

The road wound this way and that for about four miles. She was beginning to wonder if the sign she'd seen could possibly have been misleading. Just as she was seriously questioning whether she should go on, the road topped a small rise. The vista that spread out before her literally took Lisa's breath away.

She slowed to a stop and just stared. Ahead lay a vast open field framed by a distant pine forest beyond which lay the mountains. Across the field, just visible over the gently undulating ground, the river gleamed. The reason for its name suddenly became evident. The water was an extraordinarily clear shade of blue.

It sparkled, it danced, it fairly invited even the most hardheaded to play in it.

At intervals along the river, there were structures built of stone, glass and tile. So perfectly did they fit the landscape that they appeared almost to have grown there rather than been built.

A meadow of wildflowers extended all around and even in among the buildings, interrupted only by a few narrow roads and gravel pathways. Birds soared overhead. Deer roamed unimpeded and unafraid. It truly did look like paradise.

Or at least Lisa's idea of it. Her eyes drank it all in even as her spirit soared. What an extraordinary place. How fortunate that it was to be used wisely, protected and nurtured. That she was going to be part of that seemed just this side of miraculous.

She started the car again and drove slowly until she reached what seemed to be the main building. Parking in front, she got out and looked around again. She was still gazing about when a young man came out of the building, saw her and grinned.

"Would you be Lisa Preston?" he asked, coming toward her. He was just a couple of years older than she, of medium height, slender, with sandy hair and a pleasant, open face. When she nodded, his smile deepened.

"We were hoping you'd get here today." Holding out his hand, he said, "I'm Dave Malone. Welcome to Teal River."

"Thanks," Lisa said, holding out her own hand. "I'm delighted to be here."

"We all feel that way. How about I show you where you'll be staying? When you've had a chance to get settled, we can do the quarter tour."

"Sounds great."

They got into her car. Dave directed her a short distance to a small building standing off by itself and surrounded by a copse of birch trees. "That's yours," he said.

The house was a five-minute-or-so walk from the main part of the complex. Dave opened the door and stood aside for her to enter. Lisa stopped on the threshold and gave a soft sigh of appreciation. He laughed when he heard it.

"Really something, isn't it?" Dave said. "I had the same reaction myself when I first came here. It takes a while to get used to the fact that everything doesn't just look perfect, it actually is."

Lisa had to agree. In such a setting, there might have been a temptation to go for the overgentrified "country" look found in glossy magazines and the like. It had been resisted. The cottage was outfitted with furnishings that had a Shaker-like simplicity, glowing honey-toned woods, pure lines, everything managing to be both functional and exquisite. The result would have been somewhat austere but for the touches of what had to be original folk art—wall hangings, carvings and the like, all selected with a restrained and discerning eye.

She breathed in deeply, inhaling the scents of dried flowers, lemon polish and wood. The very air itself seemed to caress her, inside and out. A sense of contentment unlike anything she had ever known crept over her.

"Is it all like this?" Lisa asked.

Dave nodded. "No two structures are alike, yet they all feel the same way." He paused for a moment, then added, "I'll let you get settled. Come over to the main building whenever you're ready."

She gave him a smile that must have expressed what she was feeling just then. He did a quick double take. There was an odd look in his eyes, as though he'd just figured something out. He nodded once and left.

Birds were singing outside her bedroom window when Lisa woke the next morning. After years of waking to the sounds of traffic, she just lay there and listened for a while. The air had the same fresh, enticing scent as the day before. Coming in through the windows she'd left partly open, it seemed to beckon her outside.

She went but not before having a nice long, hot shower and a cup of tea, courtesy of the fully equipped kitchenette nestled away in a corner of the main room. She had stayed up long enough the previous evening to unpack, then gone to bed while it was still early.

She hadn't really expected to fall asleep, but the

events of the past week must have taken an even greater toll than she'd thought. Before she knew it, she was waking to her first full day at Teal River.

She couldn't let herself wonder how many more of them there would be. Already, she was in love with the place. As promised, Dave had shown her around before she joined him and several other members of the staff for dinner in the common room. The food was delicious but the camaraderie was even better.

Everyone was relaxed and friendly, no one trying to impress anyone else, and no one seemingly in the least perturbed that an outsider had been brought in to handle promotion. Lisa had answered a few friendly questions about her work, and that was that.

Afterward, she'd gone for a brief walk alone, following one of the paths down to the river's edge. Sitting there with her knees tucked up under her chin, she felt a universe away from the cares that had weighed her down such a short time before.

And now, with sunlight sparkling and a fresh breeze blowing, she felt capable of tackling anything. Her step was light and she was smiling as she walked over to the main building where an office had been set up for her.

Although she was still glad that she'd brought her notebook computer, the state-of-the-art desktop model provided for her was a joy to behold. Her appreciation deepened even further when she realized it came fully equipped with all the latest bells and whistles for graphics, desktop publishing, Net access and the like.

Knowing that she could get very into playing with
that thing, she decided to check out the rest of the
office first. Somebody—and she would have to find
out who it was so that she could make the proper
thank-yous—had guessed that great as the computer
was, she would want to be able to get her hands dirty.
The assortment of art materials was almost too much.
Almost. It was going to be a real toss-up which to
wallow in first—the computer or all the rest.

What a very nice problem to have, Lisa thought
with a grin. Mary hadn't been kidding when she'd
said her luck was about to change. It had done so
with a vengeance.

She was still thinking about that when she headed
for the common room to join Dave and the others for
a working lunch. So absorbed was she in her thoughts
that she didn't notice the man who stood some distance away from the building, watching her as she
walked along the glass-lined passage.

She was here. He'd known that the previous day,
of course, having been informed as soon as she arrived. But it hadn't fully registered until he saw her.

Tad leaned up against the trunk of a willow tree
and watched Lisa until she was out of sight. She
looked very young, very happy and every bit as beautiful as he remembered. Actually, a little more.

Just seeing her made him smile, but that didn't last
long. She was going to be tearing mad when she realized he was here. And when she found out exactly

what he had to do with Teal River, "mad" probably wouldn't get close to describing how she felt.

He just had to hope that by then she was too committed to the project to back out. It would be a challenge for her, the kind of thing she loved to do, and she was more than up to it.

Pride alone had made him determine all that before arranging for her to be offered the job. If it hadn't worked out, he would have thought of something else, but as it was, circumstances seemed to be fitting together in his favor.

Or at least they were until Lisa found out the truth. Then it was anyone's guess what would happen.

He grimaced as he straightened away from the tree and began walking back down an almost-concealed path that led away from the main complex. About a quarter mile beyond it, he came to his own house.

As with all the structures at Teal River, it was built of stone, tile and glass. Nestled into the curve of a hill that rose above the river, the house enjoyed an unparalleled view.

Before the building itself—or any of the others—existed, Tad had camped on the site, finding in it a rare chance to escape from the demands of his life. It wasn't an exaggeration to say that he'd conceived the idea of a resort-development company dedicated to preserving the natural environment right where he was standing. That it would go on to become what it had would not have occurred to him.

He shook his head a little wryly. News of his retirement from the music business wouldn't really make any difference. He would probably always be seen in that role. But the reality was that the bulk of his personal fortune—and his interest—was rooted now in sane, wise development of natural resources.

Almost ten years since he'd begun buying up the land along the Teal River, he was ready to bring all his skill and experience to bear to create the place he had only dreamed of before.

That should have been enough for him. He should have been completely absorbed by it to the exclusion of all else.

And so he might have been, were it not for Lisa Preston.

Acknowledging that, even in the privacy of his own thoughts, freed the anger he'd been struggling to ignore. He couldn't anymore. It was there, all right, just below the surface—anger directed at the utterly unexpected and unknown force that had come into his life.

He had never pursued a woman. That admission, even to himself, embarrassed him somehow. But it was true nonetheless and he had to face it. The circumstances of his life had been such that there had never been any reason to court, cajole or otherwise seduce a woman.

Until now.

What in heaven's name was wrong with him? Why hadn't he been able to forget her? She had teased him unbearably, then played the offended virgin, of all things, and when he'd tried to apologize anyway, she'd damn near hung up on him.

In return, he'd set out to learn everything he could about her, dangled before her a job he knew she wouldn't be able to resist, and even instructed his staff not to mention his name to her, all for the sole purpose of bringing her under his—

Control?

That was absurd. Women weren't controlled. They were equal partners in every way, holding down jobs, caring for families—often alone, doing everything men did and probably more.

Bringing her into his world?

That was better. He'd done everything he needed to in order to bring Lisa into his world where he hoped they would both get to know each other better. Where they could discover whether this strange compulsion he felt for her might by any remote chance be returned. And if there was anywhere for it to go.

He ran a hand through his raven hair and sighed. There were people who would fall down laughing so hard they would hurt themselves if they knew of his predicament. There were women, in particular, who would think it the sweetest justice.

And then there was Lisa—

He had no idea what she would think, feel or do, once she found out who he was.

Moreover, he'd just discovered that he wasn't in all that much of a tearing hurry to find out.

Let her settle in first. Yes, that sounded like a good

idea. Let her fall in love with Teal River. Then, perhaps she would—

A hard, mirthless smile curved his mouth. This was not about love. Love didn't exist except between parent and child, perhaps. This was about lust. Good, old-fashioned, stomach-clenching, reason-banishing lust.

Hot, hard lust.

Nothing more.

Having clarified that in his own mind, he continued on toward the house. He would give Lisa a few days, perhaps even a week. That decision pleased him. He was a patient man and in control of himself—all evidence not to the contrary.

A week.

Unbidden, his body told him what it thought of that.

He sucked in air and laughed, very faintly. All right, not a week. A few days...four or five.

Two or three.

One.

Chapter 6

Perhaps because she'd gone to bed so early the previous night, Lisa had trouble falling asleep. Or perhaps it was just that she was so excited and happy.

And troubled.

That last part had crept up on her throughout the day but she'd been far too busy to realize it. Everyone she met had something new to tell her about Teal River, always with great enthusiasm and sincerity. Everyone wanted to show her another part of it.

The more she heard and saw, the more she realized what a truly dream project this was. It was the kind of job guaranteed to garner attention, the kind that could make a career or even the success of an agency. Any number of her colleagues would have killed for it. Would, for that matter, have done it gratis simply to have the credential.

And it had fallen into her lap along with a nice, fat paycheck.

It didn't figure.

She hated thinking that way, but honesty was forcing her to do so. No matter what Mary had said, and what Lisa herself knew to be true, there was no reasonable explanation why she'd been hired without even the usual interviews.

It would have been perfectly acceptable for her to be asked to produce sample ideas, even work them up to some extent. The explanation that her work had already been seen and approved just didn't hold up.

So what was she doing here?

Other than entertaining slightly paranoid fantasies, of course.

She sighed ruefully and wiggled deeper under the covers, trying without success to get comfortable.

It was almost midnight. She had another very full day on tap for tomorrow. She had to get some rest. But try though she did, sleep remained elusive. Finally, she gave up and left the bed.

The thought of a warm bath tempted her, but she'd already bathed in the oversize whirlpool, lingering far longer than she would have normally, just for the sheer pleasure of it. After years of living in apartments with only showers, or at most dinky little tubs that couldn't even accommodate all of her long legs, the whirlpool was a delight. Her toes were definitely pruney before she finally left it.

There was always warm milk. The kitchenette was

small but well-equipped, including the contents of the half-size refrigerator. But warm milk made her want to gag and she wasn't in the mood for cocoa.

Some fresh air, then. The night was cool but not unpleasantly so. She wrapped a thin silk robe around herself and stepped out onto the porch. From where she stood, she could see the curve of the river glowing in moonlight. For a brief moment, she wondered if she would ever become accustomed to such beauty. Could it ever become ordinary?

The thought amused her. She laughed softly and leaned against the porch rail. It was as she did so that she caught a glimpse of something moving in the trees near the river. She looked more closely.

A tall, very broad-shouldered man was walking by the water.

Why not? There were a dozen or more men working at Teal River. She'd met them all since her arrival and while she might still be sorting out a few names and faces, she'd found them perfectly pleasant.

Why, then, did she instinctively draw back into the shadows of the porch, watching the man as he drew nearer? He really was very tall, even more so than she'd thought at first glance, and heavily muscled. Offhand, she couldn't recall any of the men she'd met who looked like that. He moved with easy grace and did not seem at all discomfited by the darkness.

Her breath caught as it seemed that he was going to come right to her cottage. But he stopped while still some distance away and merely stood, looking directly at her. Her heart thudded in her throat. She was certain he must be able to see her until she remembered the deep shadows in which she stood. If she didn't move, she would be invisible to him.

He turned to go. For just an instant, she saw him in profile. At the same moment, the moon emerged from behind a cloud and shone directly on him. The gasp that would have torn from her was only stopped by her hand pressed hard against her mouth. Seen from the side, the man's aquiline features were shockingly familiar, as was the unmistakable outline of a neat queue gathered at the nape of his neck.

Tad.

It had to be.

It couldn't be.

She was overly tired, too excited by the new job.

She was prey to a fantasy.

Perhaps she was even asleep in her bed and simply didn't realize it.

Another cloud drifted across the moon. She strained her eyes, trying desperately to see him again. But when the ribbon of silver light emerged once more, the field in front of the cottage was empty.

There was nothing at all to see there.

Despite everything, Lisa slept. But not well and not for very long. She woke to soft gray light and the realization that dawn was still some time off.

Resolutely, she closed her eyes and tried to sink back into sleep. It wasn't to be. After a few minutes, she gave up and, grumbling, left the bed. A quick shower and a cup of coffee later, she stepped outside.

Later, she supposed she would regret not getting more rest but the soft, fresh day was too enticing to resist. It was already warm, making her glad that she hadn't bothered with more than jeans and a loose silk shirt tucked in at the waistband. Dress among the staff of Teal River was decidedly casual, even more so than anywhere else she had worked. She was glad of it, not being inclined to formality.

She'd left her hair down and done no more than wash her face. With an easy step, she walked toward the river. Since her arrival, she had been too busy meeting people and settling in to really pause and enjoy her surroundings. Now she was determined to do so.

She followed the river where it curved and came to a part of the complex she hadn't seen before. On a rise to her left stood a house. It was made from the same materials as her cottage—stone, tile and glass— but the effect was altogether different.

Whereas the cottage was comfortable and cozy, the house seemed to rise proudly from the land that cradled it. Every line, every angle had been crafted by a master hand. An entire wall of windows looked out beyond the river and meadows to the majestic mountains. Lisa caught herself imagining what it would feel like to stand there and watch a storm whip over the mountains, or see the sun rise, or simply gaze at the stars.

Dave hadn't mentioned anyone beyond the people she had already met but the resort development company must have high-ranking executives. One of them had apparently taken advantage of his position to create the magnificent residence.

Thinking of that unknown executive reminded her of the doubts she'd been having regarding how she'd been picked for the job. Although neither Dave nor anyone else had said so, she supposed that eventually she would meet some of the higher-ups. Certainly, they would be paying very close attention to Teal River and everything that went on there.

She was wondering how long it would be before she had to deal with the management types when a sound drew her up short. Above the gentle rush of the river, she heard a much louder splash, as though something had just hit the water.

But when she looked around, she saw nothing. Quickly, she continued along the riverbank until she came to an abrupt stop. Directly ahead of her the river widened. No, that was misleading. It ran alongside a rock-lined pool that was fed by an underground stream that joined the river just beyond the pool. A light mist rose from water that looked almost silver and twined through the branches of the pine trees that all but encircled the sylvan glade.

Someone was in the pool. As she watched, a large, dark shape cut through the water. A swimmer—one with a great deal of skill and power.

Unbidden, the memory of what she thought she had

seen from the porch the night before rose to taunt her. She took a quick step back but couldn't contain a small exclamation of surprise and burgeoning distress.

Almost anywhere else it would have gone unheard. But Teal River was solitude and serenity, the peace of nature untrammeled by more than minimal human interference.

Sound carried.

The swimmer paused, came upright in the water. Lisa had a sudden terrible urge to flee. It took a conscious act of will to remain where she was standing. To do otherwise would be childish in the extreme. She was on the verge of making a fool of herself. Someone was swimming. What of it?

A man. The figure rising from the water was clearly male. The shoulders and chest were massive, the torso tapering down to lean hips and...

She looked away quickly. Even in the faint light, she could see that the man hadn't bothered with a bathing suit. Her face heated. She was violating his privacy. She had to go.

She stayed right where she was. She didn't even blink as he reached for the towel he'd left beside the pool and wrapped it around his taut waist.

The sun was rising, turning the eastern horizon blood red. The sky lightened. Where before there had been only soft tones of gray and silver, color began to emerge. The skin stretched tautly over the man's powerful muscles and sinews was bronzed. His hair

was pure black, long enough to touch his shoulders,
untamed. He turned and—

"*No!*"

Lisa didn't realize she had spoken out loud until
she heard her own voice. It was too late. The man
had also heard. He went very still and looked directly
at her.

The same light that had revealed him banished the
shadows where she had been hidden. She stood, shorn
of concealment, fully exposed to his gaze.

Slowly, he walked toward her.

Chapter 7

"Hello, Lisa," Tad said quietly. Unlike her own voice that had sounded harsh in the morning stillness, his was low and muted.

She took a quick step back, caught herself doing it and stopped. A strange sense of unreality settled over her. She wanted desperately to believe that she was caught in a dream even as she knew she was not.

"What are you doing here?" she asked.

He sighed and ran a hand through his thick, dark hair. It was wet from his swim. Droplets of water flew off his fingers. His eyes were shuttered, his expression revealed nothing.

"Teal River belongs to me." He smiled slightly and added, "As much as a place as beautiful and free as this can ever truly belong to anyone."

"I see...." She didn't but she was beginning to, and she didn't like what she thought she saw. Not at all. "The resort-development company..."

"Mine. I started it a few years back with profits from the music business."

"Oh, yes, the music business." The anger growing in her put a hard edge on those words. "I must have seemed incredibly naive, not knowing who you were. I imagine you had a good laugh over it."

He didn't comment on that but merely shrugged those impossibly broad shoulders, the same ones she remembered clinging to in the heated moments they had shared. But he'd been dressed then, and he was barely that now. The difference sent a wave of heat through her, reminding her of exactly how susceptible she was to this man.

"Actually, nothing involving you has provided me with any amusement," he said.

She stared at him for a long moment. The reality of his presence there right in front of her stunned her. She could barely comprehend it.

Teal River was his. That much she understood. Much as she would have liked to believe her being hired to do the promotion for it was merely an outrageous coincidence, she didn't let herself think that for an instant.

"Why did you do this?" she asked. Her hands were clenched at her sides.

Realizing it, she forced herself to release them. Standing very straight and tall, she refused to let him see the storm of confusion, dread and something perilously close to excitement that he had unleashed in her.

He hesitated. She took some very scant satisfaction from that, but it was fleeting, gone in a moment.

"I was curious about you," he said. "It wasn't difficult to find out what you did for a living, or that you're very good at it." He shrugged again, as though none of this was of any importance. "There didn't seem to be any reason not to offer you a job for which you were obviously well qualified."

"No reason except that there are hundreds of other equally qualified people."

He smiled faintly, as though her candor *did* amuse him. "Not hundreds." Provokingly, he added, "Ten or twenty, maybe."

She shook her head in disgust, not even so much at him as at herself. What an idiot she'd been!

"I did wonder why I wasn't even interviewed. But I actually let myself think the whole thing was just dumb luck. How incredibly stupid."

She took one last, long look at him, not even resisting the pain that twisted through her. She deserved it for being so deep-down dumb. Abruptly, she turned on her heel and walked away.

She got no more than half-a-dozen steps. The hand that closed on her arm wasn't hurtful, but it was very strong and very unyielding. Her breath caught as she was drawn toward him, close enough to feel the heat of his almost-nude body without actually touching.

"There's no reason to be upset," he said, very low. "You want this job. You know that. And you'll do it very well."

She twisted, trying to pull loose, but succeeded only in reminding them both of how easily he could stop her.

"No, I won't," she said. He was far bigger and stronger than she was, and he was obviously far too used to getting his own way. But Mr. Tad Jenkins was about to learn a lesson he badly needed. She took some vengeful pleasure in teaching it to him.

"I won't be doing any sort of job at all," she said. "I'm leaving."

He didn't respond at once. Or perhaps he did, but not verbally. His hold on her arm tightened fractionally, then abruptly eased. He didn't let go of her, but she had the sense that he was making a conscious effort not to hurt her.

"You're forgetting something," he said expressionlessly.

"What?" She would not let him see how he was affecting her. She absolutely would not.

"You signed a contract."

Her gaze flew to his face. He couldn't possibly be serious. Contracts were completely routine in such situations. Mary had checked it over, pronounced it fine, and Lisa had signed without a second thought. Now she had cause to regret that. "Tear it up."

The smile was back, the one she was rapidly learning to detest. He let go of her suddenly and even put a small distance between them. Not much; just enough to let her breathe a little more freely.

"Not a chance," he said.

Anger flared in her. He looked insufferably calm, as though her wishes were of no more concern to him than the fluttering of the breeze. "Tear it up," she repeated through gritted teeth.

His gaze leveled on her. She barely managed to suppress a shudder. What she'd thought was calm was in reality cold, hard will.

"The fact that we happen to have some nodding acquaintance doesn't affect the terms of the contract between us at all. Every stipulation your agent insisted on—on your behalf—regarding salary, working conditions and so on has been met. You have no excuse for reneging and if you try to—"

"You'll what?" she demanded angrily. Dammit, he was not going to intimidate her! He was a rude, manipulative, deceitful lout who undoubtedly thought he was God's gift to women. But she'd told him the truth—she wasn't some little groupie and she wasn't about to act like one.

"Sue me?" she continued, her voice thick with derision. "Or wreck my career, fix it so I can't work? Well, let me tell you something—"

"I'll be very disappointed in you," he said, very quietly.

She stopped cold. Oh, this really was dirty pool. What did she care what he thought of her? So what if he was "disappointed," of all things?

"You're supposed to be a professional," Tad said. "A damn good one, from what I've been told. Teal River is a tough project. We're walking a very fine line here, making some of the land available for use but only under very restricted circumstances and preserving all the rest. We have to make people want that, despite the fact that they won't have anywhere near the control they'd normally expect to have when buying a piece of property—especially so, given what they'll be paying. That won't be easy for anyone to swallow. They have to see that what they're getting will make that worthwhile."

"It will be," Lisa said without hesitation. Despite her anger at him, what he'd just said struck a powerful chord with her. She understood what he meant about people expecting to have control, but Teal River was different. It was no exaggeration to say that it was unique.

Could the same be said of the man who protected it?

Now where had that thought come from? She really had to get a grip on herself. So far as she could see, he'd had all the advantage so far. It was time for that to change.

"All right," she said. "We have a contract. I'm here to do promotion for Teal River. That's it. So long as we *both* understand that, there shouldn't be any problem."

His eyebrow rose mockingly. "Is there any other reason why you would be here?"

An unwelcome sense of embarrassment crept over Lisa but she repressed it firmly. She might not take first place for sophistication but she knew he had wanted her physically. She'd refused him and he hadn't liked that at all.

But would he really have gone so far as to lure her to Teal River with a plum job simply because he desired her? Now that she forced herself to confront that head-on, she had to admit it seemed extremely unlikely. She was attractive enough, she supposed, but she didn't fool herself. Tad Jenkins could have his pick of women. Why would he bother to pursue the rare one who'd said no?

Belatedly, she realized that he had let go of her arm. There was nothing keeping her standing so very close to him. In fact, nothing was keeping her there at all.

She thought she should say something—*Nice to see you again. So long. Good night.* Something. But the tightness of her throat warned her that trying to talk just then wasn't a good idea. Trying to sound as though she was cool, calm and collected about all this was an even worse one.

She didn't say a word. Instead, she just turned and walked away. Walked. Her pride demanded that. She was damn well not going to run.

Chapter 8

Tad watched her go. His chest felt constricted and every muscle in his body seemed to be clenched. When she was out of sight, he slumped against the nearest tree trunk and took a long, deep breath.

That helped...some.

Okay, she'd seen him, they'd talked and the roof hadn't fallen in. Of course, there didn't happen to be any roof here but he would take what he could get.

She was staying. He concentrated on that and allowed himself a small smile.

For the moment. The smile faded quickly, giving way to a more thoughtful expression. Lisa had guts, he was willing to give her that. And she was a professional. She'd obviously decided that she was going to live up to the commitment she'd made.

The commitment he'd maneuvered her into making.

He wasn't going to feel guilty about that. Everything he'd told her was the truth—she really was eminently qualified to do the job. Moreover, he fully intended to let her do it. Getting her there was as far as he went. Whatever happened next was as much up to her as it was to him.

Actually, more so. He knew what he wanted. His body had been reminding him of it ever since he first saw her standing at the edge of the pool. The problem was what she wanted—and didn't want.

She'd made her feelings crystal clear. He was honor bound to respect them.

The smile returned, deepened. He would never dream of ignoring her feelings. But that didn't mean he wouldn't do whatever was necessary to change them.

He was whistling as he walked back up to the house.

An hour later, dressed in well-worn jeans and a cotton shirt left open halfway down his chest to catch the breeze off the river, Tad entered the main building. He got himself a cup of coffee from the urn in the common room, said hello to the half-dozen-or-so people gathered there, and headed for his office. He could have worked at the house—and sometimes did—but generally he preferred being closer to the center of activity.

In his experience, most good decisions got made

not in formal meetings but as the result of casual conversations caught on the run. He encouraged what his staff laughingly referred to as "creative chaos," which meant he hired the smartest, most talented people and trusted them to do their jobs. That didn't make for the neatest, most orderly work environment, but he would have hated any such thing.

On the way to his office, he passed Lisa's. The door was open but she wasn't there. It was on the tip of his tongue to ask where she'd gone but he thought better of it. If he was going to stick to his resolve, he shouldn't show any particular interest in her.

Yeah, he could do that. Right after he stopped breathing.

With a sigh, he settled down behind the plain oak worktable that served as his desk and resigned himself to shuffling through several foot-high piles of paper. Creative chaos might do for everyone else, but someone had to wade through the stacks of government forms—federal, state *and* local—make sure the electric bill got paid on time, and generally keep things running smoothly.

He could have delegated that—and frequently was tempted to do so—but Teal River was ultimately his responsibility. He wanted to be involved in every detail of it, no matter how tedious. Indeed, he demanded that.

With a wry twist of his mouth, he remembered what Dave Malone had dubbed him not too long after the project got under way—their Designated Grown-up. There were plenty of people who had known him in his wilder days who would have split a gut at the mere thought. But that was then, this was now, and the role seemed to fit. He didn't even mind it—much.

Feeling hideously virtuous, he devoted a full three hours to plowing through the paperwork. When he finally pushed back from the worktable, he was almost caught up. Since he'd long ago decided that it was impossible to ever be fully caught up—there had to be some government regulation against it—that was good enough.

He'd earned a respite but he didn't particularly want one. What he did want was to see if Lisa had come back.

But when he looked, her office was still empty. He stood for a moment, staring at it. If she'd changed her mind and left after all, he would have been told by now. Wouldn't he?

He glanced around. Three office doors were shut— one with a Keep Out sign posted—a sure sign of frantic activity going on inside. Two informal groups were gathered in the common room, the members of one arguing, the others apparently sulking.

Tad kept going. Outside, the sun was gilding the tips of the pine trees. The air smelled as though every wildflower in the world had unleashed its perfume simultaneously. A doe raised her head and gazed at him solemnly from not more than ten feet away.

He hardly noticed. He wasn't looking for Lisa. He

had no concern at all about where she'd gone. He just wanted to take a break.

The paddocks were a short distance away from the main building. Before he reached them, he heard a familiar nickering. Diablo was racing along the railing, hooves flashing as he flew over the ground and came to a sudden stop, clumps of mud flying in all directions.

Tad laughed. He held out a bronzed hand and rubbed the stallion's velvet nose affectionately. "Missed you, too, boy."

Ten minutes later, horse and man were heading out on the trail beside the river. He couldn't remember a time when he hadn't been able to ride. His mother swore he'd been on a horse before he could walk and he believed her. He moved as one with the powerful stallion, completely relaxed and at ease.

Until he came around a bend in the trail and saw the woman sitting a short distance ahead.

Lisa was perched on a rock that jutted out over the water. Her chin rested on her knees. Her hair was in a thick braid down her back. She was dressed as he'd seen her earlier—in jeans and a loose silk shirt that was the same tawny color as her eyes. She looked very relaxed, even a little pensive.

Or she did until she heard Diablo snort. Then she raised her head and immediately stiffened. He saw that even across the distance separating them. She was instantly, acutely aware of him—and on her guard.

A sigh escaped him. He urged the horse forward

slowly, one hand on the reins, the other resting lightly at his side. He kept his gaze carefully neutral despite the pleasure it gave him just to look at her.

With a courteous nod, he said, "Nice day."

Nice day? What kind of thing was that to say? He sat there on that magnificent horse—looking unbearably masculine and darkly handsome, like something out of a fantasy—and he said, "Nice day"?

Lisa stood. She wasn't thinking too clearly—all right, not clearly at all—but she could still figure out that it was a smart idea to stay on her feet around him. Her palms were sweating. She pressed them against the sides of her legs and hoped he didn't notice.

"Yes, it is," she said.

He wanted superficial? She would give him superficial. She would even throw in a little banal. "Feels like it might rain later."

He nodded again, slowly. "Might."

She nodded slowly. "Nice horse."

"Thanks. His name's Diablo."

It would be. The horse looked as though he would as soon trample her as stand there pawing the ground and snorting. She'd never been afraid of horses, had even ridden a little. But the stallion made her nervous.

Not as nervous as the man did. Nothing came close to that.

He moved closer. Where she was standing on the rock put her at eye level with him. That was something, she supposed.

The burnished skin around his eyes crinkled. He looked as though he should be smiling, but he wasn't. Instead, he was studying her with an intensity that made it difficult to breathe. The day was very still, suddenly. She swore she could hear her heart beating.

Perhaps he could hear it, too.

Abruptly, he held out his hand in a gesture she no longer had any difficulty recognizing. He wanted something, and he was going to get it.

No, not something. Someone. Her.

"Come ride with me," he said and, without a moment's hesitation, lifted her onto the saddle in front of him.

Lisa yelped. She wasn't proud of making such a ridiculous sound but she couldn't help it. He had taken her completely by surprise. Not only did he not make any pretense of asking for permission, but he lifted her so easily—with one arm, no less. She wasn't a small woman. Slender, yes, but not small. How could he possibly have done that?

How could she possibly have let him?

"Put me down," she said, managing to sound more annoyed than frightened. That was a good trick, all things considered, and she gave herself a mental pat on the back for it.

Her satisfaction didn't last long. He ignored her and turned Diablo back toward the trail. She was left with the undignified option of struggling, and that she refused to do.

In her best scathing tone, she said, "Is there a problem with your hearing?"

His arm tightened around her just a little. "No, no problem."

"Then perhaps I wasn't clear enough. Put me down."

He hesitated. She had to give him that much. Too bad it didn't seem to make any difference. "I really should do that, shouldn't I?"

"Bingo. So what's stopping you?"

"There's something I'd like to show you."

That was what this was about? He wanted to show her something? "Did it occur to you to just ask?"

"Yes," he admitted. "And I undoubtedly should have." He bent over her slightly so that she felt his breath warm against her cheek. "I'm behaving very badly. I apologize."

Not fair. Oh, no, absolutely not fair. He had no right to make her insides go all soft and yielding like that. He was in the wrong; he'd even said so. He just didn't seem inclined to do anything about it.

"You're not going to put me down?" It was a question but she already knew the answer.

To give him credit, he phrased it very diplomatically. "We're almost there."

They weren't. It was another fifteen minutes or so before he drew rein just over a small hill. Lisa was about to take advantage of that to try to slide out of the saddle when she forgot what she'd intended and just stared.

All of Teal River that she'd seen so far was incredibly beautiful, but this...

A meadow of wildflowers stretched before her. It went on for as far as the eye could see. Thousands upon thousands of pale blue columbines, acacias, purple lupines and wild roses vied with soft white and brilliantly orange poppies. The air was heavy with their perfume. Butterflies flitted everywhere. The effect on the senses was nothing short of dazzling. Lisa took a deep, deep breath and despite herself, smiled.

"Oh, my."

Tad's chest rumbled. She felt it right through her. He was laughing.

"Really something, isn't it?" Without waiting for an answer, he dismounted easily and held out his arms to her.

Without thinking—which she most certainly should have been doing at that point—Lisa slid into them.

And all along the very long length of his very impressive body.

Now that was interesting. Her heart could actually stop and she could go on living. Of course, it had just gone into massive overdrive, the blood rushing through her body and her insides once again doing loop-the-loops.

Way down deep in what was left of her brain, a frantic voice was trying to be heard. Something about being sensible, not losing control, not being an idiot, being cool, calm, professional...

Something about that.

"God, you're beautiful," Tad said, and kissed her.

Oh, great. Really good. Way to go. He'd wanted her to feel safe and secure at Teal River, give her time to get to know him, not push, not pressure—all of that.

So what did he do?

He took her mouth ruthlessly, parting her lips for the thrust of his tongue. He stroked and savored, he nibbled and sucked, and he did it all with only the very slightest twinge of conscience.

Not that it stopped there. His hands were as well occupied as his mouth. He caressed the slender length of her back before cupping her buttocks, squeezing lightly. She moaned against him.

That was enough. Whatever noble resolve he might have mustered at that point went flying off with the butterflies. He bent slightly, put an arm under her knees and simultaneously lifted her off her feet and lowered them both onto the carpet of wildflowers.

Lisa's pupils dilated. He loomed above her, big, hard and clearly determined. She should have been screaming bloody murder, fighting him every inch of the way, but when she did manage to raise her hands it was only to clasp his broad shoulders and draw him closer.

His mouth took hers again with hungry demand before tracing a line of fire down her slim throat. His hands drew the loose silk blouse from her waistband

and slipped under it, stroking her breasts through the thin lace of her bra.

She made a soft, whimpering sound deep in her throat. Pleasure cascaded through her. It was like the evening at the hotel, only more so. Her nipples were hard before his thumbs even began to stroke them. There was a strong, rhythmic clenching in her belly that she couldn't control at all. Nor could she lie still beneath him. Her body writhed, her hips rising instinctively.

Buttons popped on her shirt. He unsnapped the front closure of her bra and she felt the sudden, warm abrasion of his skin, unshaven since early morning, against her sensitive flesh. Tremor after tremor ran through her, one rushing after another. She cried out, her head falling back.

The sky was a brilliant blue, endless, sweeping. It seemed to pulsate with the same pounding urgency driving her. She could not get close enough to him. The barriers of clothing were intolerable. When Tad raised himself slightly, watching her with hooded eyes, she unbuttoned his shirt, then pressed her bared breasts to his chest. The sensation against her tender nipples was unlike anything she had ever known. A sob broke from her. He muttered something thick, guttural, and lowered her again.

His hands were at the zipper of her jeans. She was mindless, uncaring, utterly incapable to refusing him anything. The woman she had thought herself to be was gone. In her place was an altogether different creature—sensual, demanding, carnal. All restraint had vanished. Her hands reached out, stroking him, bidding **him** to come to her even as her legs rose, open and bent at the knees, in an invitation as primal as it was unmistakable.

Tad was reaching to yank her jeans down when he suddenly froze. Through the red mist of desire so intense he thought it might kill him—and he didn't care—he realized what he was about to do.

Truly realized it.

The extraordinary affinity he had sensed between them that first night had not been an illusion. It existed, and it was even more powerful than he'd thought. Although it was completely beyond anything he had ever known, he knew to the very core of his soul that it was the source of the overwhelming, insistent passion that sprang up at the merest touch or look. The same passion that was driving them both at that very moment.

The passion Lisa had been determined to deny. And to which she was now about to helplessly succumb.

Helplessly.

He didn't fool himself for a moment. This wasn't her choice. She hadn't initiated this. She'd simply fallen prey to whatever it was they were at once sharing and being controlled by.

But when that passion was sated, if only temporarily, how would she feel? He would have given just about anything he had at that moment to be able to convince himself that she would accept what had happened and be glad of it.

The problem was, he couldn't. He knew with instinct that ran bone deep that she would experience this as a betrayal of herself. That he hadn't in any way forced her, that she had been a full and complete participant, wouldn't make any difference.

Dammit.

What an unfortunate moment to discover beyond any doubt that he did indeed possess a conscience.

And that it had no intention of keeping quiet.

Slowly, reluctantly, he drew away from her. His arousal was so extreme as to be painful. If he didn't put some distance between them immediately—

Tad stood and walked a short distance away. Even with his back to Lisa, he was vividly, agonizingly aware of her. He knew the exact moment when she realized what he had done. The small, anguished moan she gave was a knife blade through him.

"Oh, God..." she murmured. The words were wrenched from her. They carried such grief that he couldn't bear it, but turned again and moved toward her. She was trying to stand but her legs were weak and she was in real danger of falling.

Before that could happen, Tad reached her. At his first touch, she cried out and actually made to strike him. "No! Get away from me! You've done what you wanted to. Leave me alone!"

He caught her fist in his hand as bewilderment roared through him. He had?

"What are you talking about? I just realized that—"

"You're paying me back for what happened at the hotel. I called a halt then, so you did now." She took a ragged breath and raised her head, staring at him with defiant pride. "All right, we're even. Let me go."

He heard the words. He even understood them... sort of. He just had trouble accepting that she truly believed he had—

"You think I aroused you to the point where we were both maddened by it, then deliberately stopped out of some sick desire for revenge?"

Her cheeks were flushed, her eyes dark and wild. Her silk blouse and lacy bra still hung open, exposing her to his gaze. He thought she was the most incredibly desirable woman he had ever seen.

Belatedly, she recognized her condition and snatched the fabric closed. But her manner remained defiant. "Why shouldn't I think that? It's perfect. I dared to refuse the great Tad Jenkins. That's not something you're used to, is it? I should have realized you'd make me pay—"

"I don't believe this!" He roared at her. He couldn't help it. Of all the incredibly stupid, insulting, naive idiocies he'd ever heard, this one beat all.

His hands closed hard around her arms. He hauled her up against him and when she would have fought, forced her to be still. Holding her gaze, he took her hand and despite her resistance, dragged it down to the bulge between his thighs.

"Does this feel like I wanted revenge?" he demanded, his voice a harsh whisper. "You've left me aching so badly I can barely stand it. I'm one breath away from pushing you down on the ground, ripping off your clothes, and pounding myself into you until neither of us can move."

All the color fled from her face. She was suddenly ashen and trembling. Desperately, she tried to pull her hand away. For a long moment, he wouldn't let her. He held her there against him, forcing her to acknowledge what she had done to him. What they had done to each other.

Abruptly, he released her. At the sight of her very real fear, a wave of self-loathing broke over him. He'd never treated a woman like this. Never come so perilously close to losing all control. What was happening to him?

"Give me a minute," he said. His harshness was unmistakable and she flinched at it. He couldn't help that. He was fighting the most desperate battle of his life for self-control and at that precise moment, he wasn't sure he would win.

He did, but it took longer than he would have liked and by the time it was over, he was thoroughly disgusted with himself. There was no excuse, absolutely none, and he wasn't going to try to invent one.

Lisa was holding her arms, staring out over the

meadow sightlessly. Her teeth worried her lower lip. She was still very pale.

He went to her. Very gently, he said, "Let's go."

She shook her head. "I'll walk."

His face stiffened. He truly regretted what he'd done—and what he'd come so close to doing—but he wasn't about to let her be foolish because of that.

"It's too far, and you're upset. I'll take you back."

He could see that she meant to refuse again. Before she could get the words out, he lifted her and whistled for Diablo. She was on the horse, in front of him, before she realized it.

They rode back in silence. He brought her to her cottage and insisted on seeing her inside. Only once he knew she was safe there was he able to leave her.

And do what had to be done.

Chapter 9

Lisa stayed in the cottage for the rest of the day. She knew she was being cowardly but she didn't care. She felt far too fragile to deal with anyone, much less take the risk of seeing Tad again.

She tried to work, using her notebook computer, and did manage to get a few things done. But with every breath she took, her thoughts strayed to what had happened in the meadow.

And what hadn't.

He'd stopped. She understood that well enough. What she didn't really get was why.

The horrible, sick certainty she'd felt that he was only paying her back for rejecting him had faded. He'd left no possible doubt in her mind of how much he desired her.

Why, then, hadn't he—?

A pained smile flitted across her face. She certainly wouldn't have done anything to stop him. She'd been completely oblivious to any thought of restraint. In his arms, she was mindless, a creature of pure sensation craving nothing other than fulfillment.

Really great.

Well, yes, it undoubtedly would be if all that craving ever got taken to its natural conclusion. But at the moment, it felt a lot like eating dirt.

After a while, her stomach rumbled, letting her know it expected to be fed better than that. She got up wearily and went into the kitchenette. Some kind soul had restocked it with homemade soup, cheeses, fresh breads, fruit and sinful little pastries. There was even a bottle of wine. She forced herself to eat at least enough to stop the damn rumbling.

There was a television but she had absolutely no desire to watch it. The CD player was another story. She was surprised to find an excellent collection of CDs that she hadn't had a chance to notice the previous day. Several types of music were included but there was a heavy slant toward opera.

About to drop the three tenors into the player, her hand froze. It was a coincidence that the music selections reflected her own taste. Wasn't it?

She finished putting the CD on but hardly noticed when the first notes of an aria began. Walking slowly into the bathroom, she opened the cabinet and studied the toiletries she had found there. She'd used the shampoo and soap yesterday and again that morning, but now she really noticed them. They were both perfumed with heather.

Heather was her favorite scent.

She walked back into the bedroom. A bookshelf was built into the headboard of the king-size bed. She found a selection of current novels, several books about advertising that were filled with delicious gossip about the business—some of it even true—and her all-time favorite book about writing, the one she'd read maybe twenty times and would read at least twenty more.

Uh-oh.

Back in the kitchen, she took a really good look around. There was a bottle of the same wine she'd enjoyed that night at the hotel. The fruit included the exact kind of purple grapes that had accompanied dessert, and which she'd shamelessly devoured.

Big uh-oh.

Just about ready to slam herself in the forehead for being so incredibly oblivious, Lisa sat down on the couch and took a very slow breath. Either Tad Jenkins was the most incredibly thoughtful and considerate employer to ever come down the pike or...

Or?

She was in even bigger trouble than she'd thought.

He wasn't just drop-dead gorgeous, incredibly sexy, and hot enough to melt Antarctica. He was sensitive.

He noticed things—about her. He acted on them.

He surrounded her with the evidence of his attention. He made her feel valued, cared for and...

Well and thoroughly seduced.

Except she hadn't been. He'd stopped.

Did Cinderella have to deal with anything like this? Naw, probably not. Once he got her back to the palace, the prince probably turned out to be a pompous oaf with an abhorrence for pumpkin coaches and an absolute disinclination to entertain fairy godmothers.

Maybe she had a fairy godmother. Now there was a thought. Maybe it was Mary. Mary, who would give a killer shark second thoughts, a fairy godmother? That was good enough to wring a giggle from her.

She was getting giddy.

She'd never been seduced—with grapes or without. She'd avoided it for a whole bunch of reasons, all centered on a morality some people might scoff at but which she believed in absolutely.

She still did. The problem was that she was beginning to believe in other things, too. No, not believe, not quite. She was more at the hoping stage.

Hoping and wanting. She would be really dumb to forget the wanting. She plucked a grape and nibbled on it absently. Sweet heaven, she wanted Tad. There was nothing even remotely principled about that. She wanted him in every way a woman could possibly want a man. She wanted to lie in his arms, to feel the touch of his hands and mouth all over her body, to touch him in the same way—without restraint or shame—to welcome him into her, cherish and care for him, become one with him.

And she would have, except that he'd stopped.

Damn the man.

She finished the grapes. She ate two of the pastries. She listened to the three tenors four times. She took a long bath to the accompaniment of *Aïda.*

She put on one of her sensible cotton nightgowns, decided she couldn't stand the touch of it against her skin, took it off, and crawled into bed naked.

The sheets were cold. They made her shiver. Ha, she thought, something he hadn't considered. No, of course he had. He'd just meant to warm her himself.

At length, and probably undeservedly, she slept.

And dreamed of butterflies.

She was up early the next morning, leaving the cottage just after dawn. It was very quiet in the main building. No one seemed to be stirring but there was already coffee out in the common room and the makings of a simple breakfast.

She helped herself, settled out on the terrace overlooking the river, and thought about what she was going to do. Her job—to start with. Teal River was going to have the best damned promotion anyone had ever seen.

But besides that...

It had been earlier than it was now when she'd seen him at the pool. Was he there now? If she walked over there, would she find him again—naked, powerful, magnificent?

Better finish her coffee first.

She sighed and tipped her head back, letting the morning seep through her. It was too late for jaunts in the pine woods. Other early risers were filtering into the common room and then out onto the terrace. The morning was too beautiful to be inside.

Dave Malone gave her a sleepy wave and came over to join her. He had a cup of tea, a croissant and a smile. "So, how're you settling in?"

I think I'm falling desperately in love with our boss with whom I almost made hot, sweet love in the meadow yesterday.

She didn't say that. She said, "Great."

"You need anything?"

My head examined? A crystal ball so I can see what I'm getting into? Some sort of guarantee that my heart won't get shattered into a million pieces?

"I'm all set, thanks."

"Tad said he talked to you."

He said that? He didn't say where, did he? Or how? Or…anything.

"That's right, we talked."

Dave laughed, a little sheepishly. "I hope you understand we keep his involvement quiet. He wants it that way."

"Which is why no one mentioned it up front?" *So that I could have run in the opposite direction.*

"Well, yeah, kind of." The sheepish look was getting worse. He put down the tea, sloshing some of it on the table.

Lisa shot him a straight-on look, the same kind she gave her brothers when they were screwing up. Dave blushed.

"What do you mean, 'kind of'?"

"Nothing...really. Just that—" He broke off, running a hand through his hair nervously. "I probably shouldn't mention this—"

"That tears it. You've got to, now."

"Tad said not to tell you, at least not until he talked to you first." He shrugged, trying to minimize it. "I just thought that was a little strange. Like I said, we don't make a big deal about him being the head honcho here, but it's not a secret, either. Or at least it never was before."

"It isn't now," Lisa said quickly. She finished her coffee and stood. "I'd better get to work. Lots to do today."

Like figure out whether she was about to go straight off an emotional cliff on the hope that she would find out she could fly.

It was late afternoon before Lisa found out that Tad had left.

For hours, she'd anticipated seeing him again, alternating between excitement and apprehension, on tenterhooks wondering what would happen.

Realizing that nothing would because he wasn't even there was more than a letdown. It hurt.

That was crazy. Why should she hurt just because

he wasn't around? He'd gone to Los Angeles, only she wouldn't have known if she hadn't happened to overhear one of the staff mention it at the coffee bar in the common room that substituted for the proverbial watercooler.

Lisa got her latté, walked back to her office, shut the door, and sat down at the worktable. He was gone. Fine, no problem. She had tons of work to do, and it would be great not to have any distractions. That was all he was, a distraction.

A twenty-four-karat, grade-A, one-in-a-million distraction.

She worked. She actually did, and she found solace in it. If nothing else, her pride was soothed. By the time she came up for air, it was early evening. The thought of retreating again to her cottage had no appeal. Instead, she joined some of the staff in the common room for dinner. The atmosphere was relaxed and enjoyable, even if she did catch herself listening for any reference to Tad—and when he would be back. There wasn't one.

Telling herself it didn't matter, she said good-night and went for a short walk before turning in. But once in the cottage, she realized sleep was impossible. Feeling at loose ends—an extremely odd sensation for her—she flipped on the TV.

At first, nothing drew her attention. She channel-churned through the usual assortment of sitcoms, talk shows and the like. She was about to give up when her focus snapped abruptly to the screen.

The very blond hostess of a pseudonews show gave the camera a wide-eyed smile and said, "Tongues are wagging in the music industry where rumor has it that country-western great Tad Jenkins walked out on a one-hundred-million-dollar deal last week. In-the-knows at his music company hope this is just a negotiating ploy but it's hard to tell with the multiplatinum heartbreaker. Jenkins has a reputation for doing things his own way, and not much caring who gets trampled in the process. Last year, he walked out on a relationship with movie star Melanie George. This year, it just might be his fans' turn."

Cut to commercial.

Oh, great. Really wonderful. Just what she needed to hear. Melanie George was the kind of woman men got disgustingly stupid about. Tall and blond, with a body to put a centerfold to shame, she had risen to stardom on a popular TV show that featured girl spies out to save the world in bikinis. From there, she'd gone on to do a series of movies that, while panned by the critics, were box-office megahits. She showed up regularly on the covers of fashion magazines and had been voted one of the world's ten most beautiful women four years in a row.

Tad had walked out on *her?*

Or had he? Maybe that was why he'd gone to Los Angeles. Maybe he was getting back together with Melanie George.

Lisa sighed. Maybe she would just sit there and torture herself a little more.

She went to bed instead.

* * *

Everything looks better in the morning, her mother always told her. One down for Mom. Morning brought nothing except gray clouds, a headache, and the steadily growing sense that her life was spinning out of control.

Tad was still in Los Angeles. She learned that by simply asking Dave, who had no idea when he would be back.

She went back to work with a vengeance. The reality was that she was genuinely good at what she did. She'd known that before, but now she was truly grateful for it. The project was challenging enough to absorb her interest. Except for a short break to collect a sprout salad and a mug of cider for lunch, she kept at it straight through the day.

Until late afternoon, when the temptation to do a little exploring finally got the better of her.

Not exploring Teal River. As enticing as that was, she had something else in mind. With her office door closed, she logged on-line and started a Web search. Soon enough, she found what she was looking for. In fact, she found too much. Asking the computer to search for Web sites related to Tad Jenkins turned up no fewer than three thousand hits. She narrowed the search, asking for personal information only, and sat back to see what would happen.

Right before her eyes, a photograph of Tad with Melanie George on his arm materialized pixel by pixel, layer by layer, until there they were, smack-dab in front of her.

Served her right. This was what she got for being nosy.

Melanie was more or less wearing a dress that couldn't have required more than a few ounces of fabric. Maybe not even that. It could have been spray-painted on. Her blond hair tumbled artfully around her bare, tanned shoulders. Her nipples showed clearly, as did the indentation of her navel below her tiny waist. She was smiling up at Tad who appeared…amused. Yes, that was it. He looked amused.

Damn the man.

And no, she didn't want to read all about Tad and Melanie's sojourn in Cannes two years ago. But she found herself doing it anyway. Reading about the "huge fight" they'd had at La Migonette restaurant where the crème de la crème of the movie world gathered, how Melanie had accused him of sleeping with a French girl, how Tad had informed her sleeping wasn't involved, how she'd thrown a glass of wine in his face, how he'd emptied the rest of the bottle down the front of her dress.

How they'd made up later on the ski slopes at Aspen.

How they'd cruised in the Mediterranean.

How they'd fought again, Melanie crashing her Porsche into his car, terrifying the lovely Italian girl who had been with him.

Italian? When had he switched to Italians?

On and on it went. Before Melanie, he'd been involved with a series of extraordinarily beautiful and successful women from various parts of the entertainment industry. Each relationship had ended stormily, amid public denunciations that delighted the ever-hungry paparazzi and gossipmongers.

And that wasn't all. Rumor had it he'd bedded a European princess in the back of a tour bus, entertained an entire chorus line in a Greek villa, and had a favorite pair of twins flown halfway around the world while on the now legendary China tour.

For God's sake.

Not sure which she was more disgusted with—her own curiosity or the subject in general—Lisa logged off and just stared at the screen. What a fabulous world they were all living in. With almost no effort, she could find all sorts of new and imaginative ways to make herself miserable.

It was gossip, nothing more. She couldn't possibly be so dumb as to believe everything that was said or written. At the very least, it all had to be terribly exaggerated. No man could—

Yeah, he could. She didn't actually have to go to bed with Tad to know that he was an intensely sexual man. His heart-stopping virility and looks would have guaranteed an endless supply of women without the added lure of his wealth and power. There was no reason for him not to have indulged himself to the fullest.

Was there?

She caught herself chewing on her lower lip and stopped. But the doubts and questions went on, whirling through her mind until she thought she would become sick from them. She stood shakily, flipped off the computer and left her office.

It was all becoming too much for her. She had to get away for a while. She began walking with no clear idea of where she was going. It was late afternoon. Light filtering through the pine trees along the trail gave her surroundings an otherworldly feeling. The silence was so complete that it seemed a sound in itself, rushing to fill her with every breath she took.

Lisa stopped abruptly. Without realizing it, she had come to the pool where she had first seen Tad. The water was still now. She stood for a time, staring at it. A slow flush warmed her cheeks. She remembered, all too clearly, the magnificence of his lithe, muscled body, the breadth of his shoulders and chest, his lean hips and powerful thighs, as perfectly made as though sculpted by a master hand. He was startlingly beautiful just to look at, but when he touched her—

She groaned softly as a jolt of what was almost physical pain vibrated through her. Astonishment rapidly followed. How could this possibly happen? Her thoughts of him were enough by themselves to bring her to a state of such extreme arousal that she could hardly bear it. For the first time, she really let herself acknowledge the power that drove men and women to forget all else. It both awed and terrified her.

Slowly, she sat down at the edge of the pool, eased

her shoes off, and let her feet dangle in the clear, cool water. The short skirt she was wearing left most of her legs bare. She slid in a little farther, welcoming the small shock even as she shivered from it. Despite that, she still felt uncomfortably hot. She glanced around, confirming that she was completely alone. The temptation to ease into the water fully was growing.

She resisted it. There was a swimming pool near the main building that the staff used. The rock pond was Tad's, or at least she thought of it that way. His house was a short walk beyond the pines. She should leave.

She stayed. The water seemed to lose its chill as she became more accustomed to it. The stillness surrounded and enclosed her. She felt set apart from everything else, as though she had somehow stepped out of the real world into another place.

And she remained so very hot....

Before she could think better of it, she reached down, grasped the bottom of the knit top she wore, and pulled it off over her head. Her bra quickly followed. Standing, she stripped off her skirt and panties, and immediately dived into the water.

The shock was more than she'd been prepared for, and she let out a small cry. But quickly enough her body adjusted. This was heaven, she thought, as she swam slowly through the silken water. Absolute heaven. A small, guilty smile lifted her full mouth. That she'd managed to reach the ripe old age of twenty-four without ever going skinny-dipping was really too bad, but at least she was making up for it now.

She laughed softly and dived under the water. The questions and concerns that had weighed her down ever since arriving at Teal River dissolved. She felt like a child again, playful and free.

But to the man watching, there was nothing the least bit childlike about her.

Chapter 10

Tad was tired. He'd intended to stay in Los Angeles for several days. Instead, he was back, having made the trip in the shortest possible time. He didn't even try to lie to himself about why. He had a one word-explanation: Lisa.

He'd left thinking that they both needed some time to adjust to what was happening between them. He especially didn't want her to feel pressured or rushed, let alone sexually harassed by the man who was, after all, her employer. It seemed like a good time to give her a little breathing room, and give himself a chance to calm down.

So much for good intentions.

He wasn't calm. He was suddenly, acutely hard, so much so that it almost wrung a laugh from him. He

might as well be sixteen again. No, he hadn't been
this bad at sixteen. He'd had it more under control
even back then. There was no getting around it—he'd
never been like this.

She was naked. He could see the pale gleam of her
body through the water, noticed also the small pile of
clothes on the rocks nearby.

He should have stayed in the house. He shouldn't
have come out, hoping a swim in the rock pond would
help clear his thoughts.

He should turn around.

Walk away.

Give her the privacy she had every right to expect.

He stayed where he was. His body seemed determined not to obey him at all. It had developed a will
of its own—a very hard, very insistent will.

She was a good swimmer. He wasn't quite so far
gone that he didn't notice that. She looked as at home
in the water as on land. Her slim, graceful form frol-
icked much as he imagined the nymphs of ancient
legend would have. Completely unselfconscious, she
came partway out of the water, affording him an un-
hindered view of her lovely breasts, and laughed as
sparkling droplets of water cascaded down her raised
arms.

His body hardened further. Prevailing wisdom had
it that you couldn't actually die from that but he was
starting to wonder. Maybe all the cases had been
hushed up.

Interesting notion, except he couldn't hold on to it

for very long. Like every other even semi-rational thought, it was dissolving under the sheer, over-whelming heat of his need. He was down to pure instinct with maybe a few grunts thrown in.

His hands tightened on the towel he held. So pow-erful was his grip that the fabric was in danger of shredding. At that moment, Lisa saw him.

She was hallucinating. He had so dominated her every moment, waking and sleeping, that she had finally managed to conjure him from thin air.

And done a damn good job of it. The low-slung jeans below the bronzed bare chest were a very nice touch. She wouldn't have thought she had that in her. Same, too, for the unbound hair flowing to his shoul-ders, dark as midnight, and the hard, almost-predatory gleam in those to-drown-in eyes.

Her imagination was definitely working overtime.

"Hello, Lisa," the figment of that imagination said.

Uh-oh.

A talking hallucination?

No...probably not.

"You're back," she observed even as her stomach took a long, slow dive.

"Yep." He nodded pleasantly and went down on his haunches scant inches from the edge of the pool. The jeans stretched tautly over his powerful thighs. "How's the water?"

She retreated, hoping it wasn't too obvious that she was doing so but not caring enough to stop. The prob-lem with that strategy was that it took her even farther away from her clothes, but she would have to work that out later.

"It's fine—no, actually it's cold. Cold but fine. How was Los Angeles?"

She absolutely was not going to act like a blithering idiot. If he could look cool and casual under such circumstances, so could she. Except for the volcano that seemed to be going off inside her.

He shrugged those impossibly broad shoulders. "It's L.A. Planning on coming out anytime soon?"

"Why do you ask?"

"You're covered with goose bumps." His smile was utterly male. "At least, the parts of you I can see."

Which, she suspected, was a whole lot more than she would be comfortable knowing. "Fine, then. Go away and I'll get out."

"Go away? I just got here."

"If you think I'll—"

He dipped a hand in the water, testing it for himself. Frowning suddenly, he stood and shook out the towel. In a voice that brooked no argument, he said, "You'll be sick if you stay in there. Get out."

"Go away."

"No."

Standoff. He was behaving very badly, and he knew it. A gentleman would put the towel down and leave. A gentleman would respect her wishes. A gentleman would...

So who ever said he was a gentleman?

"Would you prefer for me to come in after you?" he asked, silky smooth, the very soul of compromise.

She glowered at him. Good. Anger was something he could deal with. Fear would have been different. He couldn't stand the thought of her being afraid of him.

"You're a bully," she said.

He fluttered the towel. It was more an oversize bath sheet, big and fluffy. It would wrap completely around her, the same way he would.

"A tyrant."

"I'll dry your back for you."

"Oh, there's an incentive." The water really was cold. Her legs were starting to feel numb. Not actually all *that* numb, but enough to give her a needed rationalization. Still, she hesitated. He was just so much—so much man, so much challenge; so much hot, hungering enticement. She would never come close to another man like him, presuming there even was such a thing.

"Last chance," he said and with one hand reached for the snap on his jeans.

Before he could pull them off and come in after her, Lisa relented. She swam to the edge of the pool, quickly levered herself out and reached for the towel.

He wouldn't let go of it. His eyes holding hers, he moved the towel behind her, revealing her completely. His gaze swept over her from head to toe, missing nothing. Her face flamed, but deep inside she felt a burgeoning excitement that would not be denied.

"Beautiful," he murmured and wrapped her in the towel, at the same time drawing her to him. His big hands stroked her back from the nape of her neck to the curve of her buttocks. She shivered under his touch, the cold forgotten.

"I missed you," she whispered the moment before his mouth took hers.

His kiss was long, deep, demanding. She met him without restraint. All the questions and doubts that had plagued her burned away before the sheer intensity of her need for this man who held her so tenderly, with such gentle strength. Surely he wasn't the man of gossip and rumor and innuendo, the careless pleasure-seeker who used and discarded women without thought. She couldn't reconcile that man with the man she was coming to know. They seemed to have nothing to do with one another.

Unless, of course, she was fooling herself. In which case, she was about to make the mistake of her life.

She fitted herself to him as easily as if she had been doing it for years.

His hardness brushed the apex of her thighs and belly. Her breasts moved lingeringly over his bare chest. When he groaned softly, she slipped her tongue into his mouth and dueled with his.

She was on the ground. Completely unhurt, to be sure, just surprised.

"I missed you, too," Tad said from directly above

her and pushed the towel aside. He didn't give her more than a moment to adjust to this new and much more vulnerable position. His hands cupped her breasts, the callused palms teasing her sensitive skin as the thumbs raked over her erect nipples. His mouth followed quickly, suckling her hard. She cried out, arching against him, and tried to get even closer.

The damn jeans...

"Easy," he whispered, his tongue stroking her, his hand pressing lightly between her thighs, finding the exquisitely delicate point of her desire.

His mouth was at her throat, teasing, tormenting, while his hand...

The tension spiraling inside her was unbearable. She cried out softly, her nails digging into his bare back. He made a low, guttural sound and pushed her legs wide apart.

"You're so soft," he murmured. "So sleek and hot. I want to go slowly, savor every moment of this, but—"

He didn't have to explain. She felt the same way herself. Later, there would be time for slow loving, but not now.

Mindless with need, aroused to such an extent that she teetered between pain and pleasure, she cupped his face between her hands and gazed directly into his eyes.

"Come inside me now, Tad. Please. I want you there."

* * *

To give Tad credit, he didn't curse out loud. The words were muttered under his breath and over in seconds.

Swiftly, he lifted himself off Lisa, drawing her up with him, and wrapped her completely in the towel. Just as quickly, he bent, retrieved her clothes and handed them to her.

Then he stepped in front of her, blocking her from view.

"I'm over here, honey."

Peering over his shoulder, Lisa saw a little girl emerge from the trees. She was no more than five years old, with masses of curly dark hair and huge eyes. Her face had the look of a pixie—a puzzled pixie.

"Are you going swimming?" She smiled suddenly and rushed on. "Can I come, too?"

"It's too cold, peanut," Tad said gently. He walked over to the little girl and lifted her so that she sat on his forearm. She giggled and flung her arms around his neck.

Lisa took advantage of the child's preoccupation to dart behind a tree and yank on her clothes. She was shaking all over. She was also stunned. Nothing she'd read had indicated that Tad had a child. But he clearly did, and he clearly loved her very much. The look in his eyes as he listened to whatever it was the little girl was saying was so tender that it stole Lisa's breath. She was seeing a side of him she could never have imagined.

"Who's she?" the little girl asked suddenly, staring at Lisa. There was no hostility in that. She was simply curious.

"This is Lisa Preston," Tad said. "She's a friend of mine. Lisa, this is my daughter, Natalie."

The little girl nodded pleasantly. From the security of her father's arms, she said, "Hello, Miss Preston."

At that moment, Lisa's heart melted. She couldn't have explained what caused it but there was something about the child, some hint of vulnerability, even fragility, that tore straight through her. She smiled gently. "Hello, Natalie. Please call me Lisa."

Natalie thought that over for a moment. She, too, smiled. "Lisa. That's a pretty name."

"So is Natalie. It's Russian originally, you know. In fact, there was a famous Russian ballerina whose name was Natalie. When she danced, she made people believe she had become a swan."

"I'd like to be a swan," Natalie said thoughtfully. "Would you?"

"Only if I could turn back into me again."

"Yes, that's right. I wouldn't want to not be me." She laughed and tugged on her father's hair. "Daddy would be mad."

"If I had to follow a swan around, trying to get her to brush her teeth and go to bed on time? You bet I would be. And what about when you were molting?"

"What's molting?"

"When birds lose their feathers so they can grow new ones."

"Like snakes and their skins."

"Yes, like that."

Natalie looked back at Lisa. "Daddy and I found a snakeskin in Arizona. It belonged to a rattler so it was a good thing it was empty. I have it in my bedroom."

Daddy. He was well and truly a daddy. And apparently a good one. How on earth had he kept it secret when no other part of his life seemed to have been afforded any privacy at all?

"Where's Miss Harris?" Tad asked his daughter.

"Unpacking. Can we call Grandma later? I promised we would."

"You bet. Now how about you go help Miss Harris for a little while? She might not remember where everything goes."

He set her down gently, touching his hand to her hair.

"All right," Natalie said agreeably. Her eyes strayed to Lisa. "Will you come over some time? I'll show you the snakeskin."

Lisa didn't want to presume anything but neither did she want to let the child down. "If your daddy says it's okay," she said finally.

"He will," Lisa assured her with the complete certainty of a dearly loved five-year-old. She waved a small hand and skipped off into the trees.

"She looks like a pixie," Lisa said when the child was gone. "At least, what I think a pixie would look like if I ever happened to meet one."

Tad laughed. "She can be a holy terror."

"Of course. She's a kid." She widened her eyes in mock horror. "You wouldn't want a Goody Two-Shoes, would you?"

"Heaven forbid. Lisa—"

"You don't have to explain anything."

He ran a hand through his thick hair, the same hair she had grasped in the throes of passion. *Unfulfilled* passion that still resonated deep within her.

"I think I'd like to," he said and did.

Natalie was five years old; Lisa had been right about that. She'd been off visiting Tad's mother in Arizona. He'd stopped there on the way back from L.A. to collect her. He was, as the term went, the "custodial parent," with full custody.

"Her mother and I weren't married," he said quietly. "I didn't know anything about Natalie until I got a letter from a lawyer demanding child support."

"What did you do?"

"Turned it over to my lawyers. It wasn't the first time a woman had claimed to have a child I'd fathered. That kind of thing is pretty much an occupational hazard once you become well-known. Only in this case, it turned out to be true—maybe."

"Maybe?"

He shrugged. "The timing was right, Natalie's coloring made it possible. I could have asked for DNA tests but I didn't see the point."

"You just paid?"

"Not exactly." His hands fisted at his sides. A

pulse sprang to life in his tightly clenched jaw. "It seems her mother and I met during one of the very few times when Patricia was off drugs. Too bad it didn't last. Natalie was born addicted to cocaine. It was touch and go whether she'd live."

Lisa pressed her lips tightly together. That beautiful, smiling child.

"Patricia gets a very generous monthly payment in return for giving me full custody. I would have preferred to make it a lump sum and have her gone for good, but this way I can be sure she'll never come near Natalie again. She doesn't care anything about her but she values the money highly."

He laughed—a mirthless sound that made Lisa flinch. "The first few months were the toughest. Once she was home from the hospital, I kept waking up every hour on the hour, afraid she might have died. I hired live-in nurses, but I couldn't stand leaving her alone. She was so small and helpless."

"She's lucky to have you."

He shook his head. "I'm lucky. She made it, and the doctors say now that there aren't any long-term effects. She's smart as a whip, can do everything she should be doing at this stage, and frankly runs circles around me."

"You don't seem to mind."

"No, I don't. She made me realize what was really important in life. I'm not saying I got it all at once. I didn't. But I did know right from the beginning that I'd do anything I had to in order to protect her."

Lisa believed him. It was impossible not to, especially when she'd seen the evidence for herself. "Do you mind my asking how you managed to keep her existence a secret?" she asked.

"It's not...exactly. A few people know—my mother, lawyers, now you. But I've definitely kept her out of the public eye. She wouldn't be able to have any kind of normal life otherwise."

"I never really thought about it," Lisa said. "But it must be awful to know that anything you say or do is going to be taken as fodder for gossip."

"You get used to it." No sooner had he said that than he shook his head. "No, you don't. At least, I never did. But after socking a few paparazzi, I realized that wasn't getting me anywhere. The vultures have to be fed, so I fed them. I just kept them clear of Natalie."

"Melanie and the rest..." She spoke without thinking and would have given just about anything to have the words back. Too late.

His mouth thinned sardonically. "I thought you didn't know anything about me?"

She was going to have to confess. Much as it galled her, she didn't see any way out of it, short of lying to him, which she would not do.

"I did a Web search."

His eyebrows rose. "On me?"

"'Fraid so. Say, are Melanie's dresses actually sewn or are they just sprayed on?"

He thought for a moment. "Sometimes she'd have

them wet down in strategic places with a plant mister right before being photographed."

Lisa's jaw dropped. "You're kidding?"

"'Fraid not," he mimicked her. "What else did you find out?"

She was genuinely embarrassed now, but it was too late to back out. "That you like...variety."

"You think so?"

"Well, you know, the chorus line, the twins, so on and so forth—it does sort of create that impression."

He stared at her for a moment before he laughed. And laughed...and laughed. He laughed so hard she thought he was going to fall over.

"You believed it," he said when he could talk again. "You swallowed all of it."

Lisa planted her hands on her hips and glared at him. "I know perfectly well the media exaggerates, but you're not going to tell me none of it was true."

"No," he agreed, sobering, "I'm not. Some of it was, but the twins, the chorus line..." He started laughing again.

"Fodder for the vultures," she finished for him.

"It got to be a game, trying to find something so outlandish they couldn't possibly believe it. I never did."

"The European princess?"

"Well, no, that one was true."

She gulped.

He wrapped a steely arm around her waist and

hauled her up hard against him. Laughter rumbled in his chest. "Gotcha."

"I'm gullible," she moaned.

"That's okay."

"No, it isn't. It's not safe to be gullible around you." Actually, it wasn't safe being around him, period, but she wasn't going to get into that right then. She still hurt from wanting him and with each passing moment, she was feeling a real need to put some distance between them, if only temporarily.

"I'm going," she said, disentangling herself from him. She succeeded only because he let her, and they both knew it.

Chapter 11

He came a few hours after dark. Lisa was waiting for him. The scent of heather clung to her skin and hair. She wore an apricot silk nightgown that reached no farther than her mid-thighs and was scooped low over her breasts. The covers of the bed were turned down.

She wasn't going to indulge in any pretended surprise or reluctance. They both deserved more honesty than that.

She had left the lights off in the cottage but lit several candles that glowed softly and put a match to the fire she'd found already laid. When he knocked, she was sitting on the couch, staring into the flames. She rose gracefully and went to open the door.

For a moment, they did no more than look at one

another. He wore the same jeans but with the addition of a shirt. She felt a little tug of regret at that and smiled. His hair was slightly damp from a recent shower.

He looked very big, very male, and very determined.

She stood aside and said softly, "Come in."

Without taking his eyes from her, he stepped inside, shut the door behind him and locked it.

Somewhat to her surprise, he didn't reach for her. Instead, he glanced around the cottage. He could see the bedroom from where he stood, and the turned-down bed. What looked very much like relief flitted across his face.

Hard on it came desire.

His hands were gentle as he drew her to him but she wasn't misled. He was as close to being out of control as she had seen him. The waiting had been agony for them both.

Still, he hesitated, doing nothing more than hold her. She could feel his labored breath beneath her cheek. Feel, too, the waves of heat coming off him. He was all hard muscle and sinew held barely in check by a will that could not possibly last much longer.

A tiny flicker of fear tried to come to life within her. Lisa extinguished it firmly. Whatever lay ahead, she had absolutely no doubt about the rightness of this.

Taking his hand, so much bigger than her own, she led him into the bedroom.

His hot, seeking mouth tugged at her nipple. Lisa moaned frantically, twisting beneath him. They had just barely made it to the bed. Tad was still fully dressed except for the boots he'd managed to tug off. Lisa's nightgown was still in place, sort of. He'd pulled it down far enough to bare the breasts he was presently enjoying.

His big hands squeezed the pale, rose-crested globes together, allowing his mouth to move from one to the other and back again. He teased her with his tongue and lips, then lightly raked his teeth over her, making her cry out.

The intense arousal she had experienced by the pond was back in full force and increasing second to second. So profound was it that tiny flares of light were going off behind her eyes. She dragged in air, struggling to breathe, and sobbed his name.

He raised his head, his features taut. In a voice made harsh and rasping by his own need, he said, "This should be slow and gentle, sweetheart. But it isn't going to be. I just can't manage that this time."

Dazed, barely able to hear him, Lisa could only answer with her body. Again, she raised her hips in a plea that was unmistakable.

He gave a low groan and reached down to swiftly free himself. Taking both her hands in one of his, he stretched her arms out above her head. With his other hand, he pulled up her nightgown to her waist and touched the silken folds between her thighs. She was wet, swollen and hot, ready for him.

"Thank God," he breathed harshly and positioned himself to enter her. At the first touch of him, Lisa gasped. Circumstances had been such that she really hadn't seen him fully. Now, belatedly, she realized how very big he was.

Not that there was time to do anything about that. He moved within her, pushing, and muttered under his breath.

"You're small.... Easy...don't stiffen against me.... Easy, babe..."

The words didn't matter so much as the sound of his voice, oddly soothing to her. He pushed farther and a soft whimper broke from her throat. She couldn't help it but Tad was beyond hearing. He reared back suddenly, released her hands only to clasp her hips tightly, raising her to him and holding her immovable, and plunged deep inside her.

Panic roared through Lisa, almost but not quite banishing passion. She held her breath in the expectation of pain but when it came it was so much less than she'd feared. It was gone in an instant, replaced by an incredible sense of fullness that yielded in turn to a surge of pleasure that finally did make her scream.

Tad went absolutely still. She could see the disbelief stamped on his face, in his eyes, in every particle of his being.

"My God," he groaned. "I don't believe this."

To her dismay, he began to withdraw from her.

"No!" Without hesitation, Lisa levered herself up just enough to keep him inside. "You can't," she whispered brokenly. "Don't leave me like this."

He hesitated. Obeying instincts she had never known she possessed, she drew him deeper into her. The sensation of hot, steely velvet impaling her unleashed cascading shimmers of pleasure. She stroked her hands down his muscled back to his hard buttocks, urging him even closer.

She knew the very moment he surrendered. Slowly, with aching care that brought tears to her eyes, he began to move within her. His first thrusts were slow and gentle but as the pleasure built for them both, the rhythm changed, becoming much faster and deeper. Utterly caught up in it, Lisa moved with him—her back bowed, her body opening to him without restraint. A fine sheen of perspiration slicked her skin and his. She opened her eyes, seeing him above her, and let the riptide take her.

Tad lay on his back, holding Lisa tightly against him. One arm was wrapped around her shoulders, the other lay just beneath her breasts. A steely leg was thrown over both of hers. She was naked. He had stripped off her nightgown and thrown it to the floor. At the same time, he had quickly yanked off his own clothes so that there were no longer any barriers between them. He didn't question his need to keep her like this.

She had not stirred or spoken, and he was afraid to do either. He wanted to hold on to this moment forever. Nothing could have prepared him for what had happened. After years of savoring some of the most beautiful and uninhibited women in the world, he had just had the most intensely erotic experience of his life with a virgin.

Since he'd first become sexually active—way back when—he had made it a point to avoid virgins. In high school, there had been some particularly obnoxious jerks who bragged about the girls they claimed to have deflowered. Tad thought they were pathetic and gave them wide berth. He told himself that he simply preferred girls who knew what they were doing, but the reality was that he didn't want the responsibility of initiating anyone.

Later, once he was out of school, virginity simply hadn't been an issue. It wasn't around anymore. That suited him perfectly. Enough years—and enough women—had gone by that the very idea of virginity never even occurred to him. If it had, it would have seemed quaint and old-fashioned, part of another world.

Until now. Lisa was twenty-four years old and beautiful, with a warm, natural loveliness unique to herself. She'd been out on her own with a job, an apartment, all the usual accoutrements. And she'd cer-

tainly been dating. Hadn't she told him the first day
they met that she'd just broken up with her boyfriend?

So why the hell had she been a virgin?

He drew a ragged breath and schooled himself to
calm. There was no point getting angry, and certainly
not at her. Besides, if he was going to be at all honest,
he had to admit that he was having some decidedly
unenlightened thoughts on the subject. He liked—*really* liked—the idea that no other man had ever been
with her. It stirred something very primitive and pos-
sessive in him, but it also made him feel undeniably
tender toward her.

It was that tenderness that prompted him to ease
his hold just enough to turn her onto her back. Her
eyes were closed but she wasn't asleep. The rapid
beat of her heart told him that.

Carefully, he lifted himself away from her and went
into the bathroom. A moment later, he returned with
a wet cloth. His hands were very gentle as he spread
her thighs and began to wash her.

Lisa jerked upright, almost coming off the bed.
"What are you doing? No...don't..."

He pressed her back down onto the bed with one
hand while he kept the other firmly between her legs.
"Relax," he said. "This will make you feel better."

The look she gave him suggested she didn't agree,
but at least she stopped resisting. Lying back against
the pillows, she let him do as he wished. Before he
was done, soft tremors were raking her and her nipples were hard.

He took note of that before tossing the cloth aside and rising from the bed once again. In the kitchenette, he opened the small refrigerator, found the bottle of wine, and brought it back to the bed along with two glasses and a corkscrew.

Lisa sat up. She tried to draw the sheet over herself but he wouldn't let her. Instead, he handed her a glass of wine and lightly touched the rim of his own glass to hers. Very softly, he said, "Thank you."

Her startled glance was completely endearing. She looked positively flummoxed. For a moment, he was afraid she might cry. She didn't but it was close. Hesitantly, she said, "I thought you might be angry...or that you just wouldn't care."

"Wrong on both counts." He took a swallow of the wine and willed himself not to touch her. There would be time for that later. "However," he added, "I wouldn't mind an explanation."

Even by the flickering light of the candles near the bed, he could see her flush. "I'm not sure there is one," she said very low. "I had the usual urges, got the usual pressure, but I didn't want..."

"Didn't want what?" he pressed gently.

"Didn't want it to be with just anyone. I wanted it to matter." She looked away, embarrassed.

Tad let his breath out very slowly. He was riding an emotional roller coaster from exultation to humility and back again. No one had to tell him how unpredictable that made his actions, even to himself.

"I hope you feel you made the right decision," he

said, and waited through what felt like an eternity for her small but firm nod.

"Yes, I did."

Pretty good trick, being ten feet tall and still fitting in the bed. He resisted the impulse to tell her that, not feeling quite ready to joke, and instead touched her arm lightly.

"It still would have been a good idea to tell me. I would have been more careful with you."

But even as he spoke he had to wonder, would he have? His hunger for her was so great that he had to doubt whether even the knowledge of her innocence would have slowed him. Still, he had tried, however belatedly, and he found some comfort in that.

He took her wineglass and set it on the table beside his. She glanced at him uncertainly but made no attempt to pull back. The back of his hand stroked her arm once, twice, again. She shivered under his touch.

He moved a hand around to the small of her back and gathered her closer. Against the curve of her cheek, he murmured, "Tell me now if you're too sore."

Lisa turned over slowly. She wasn't absolutely sure that she wanted to but it was still nice to know that she actually could move. The smile that curved her mouth was slow, soft and fully female. Languidly, she stretched.

The sheets felt cool and smooth all along her nakedness. She stretched again, savoring the feel of them. Her body felt alive in a way it had never been before. She was vividly aware of every sensation, every impulse. Her lips were swollen, her nipples peaked for so long that they ached slightly. And between her legs...

Tad was asleep beside her. She propped herself up on one elbow and looked at him. He appeared younger and somehow less formidable, as though the rampaging male force that was so much a part of his waking being was temporarily quiescent. Thick, dark lashes fanned his high cheekbones. His nose was arrogantly straight, his mouth softened now with lips slightly parted. His chin was firm with just the hint of a cleft in the middle. He needed to shave but she'd already known that, the sensitive skin of her breasts and between her thighs being slightly abraded by his roughness.

Not that he'd been anything but gentle the second time. As though in repentance for his earlier lack of control, he made love to her with maddening slowness, teasing and tempting her until she was mindless with need. Not until she cried out for him, demanding and begging all at once, had he finally come within her. The wait had been worthwhile, her climax deep and endless.

She wasn't sore, as she'd promised him, but she did feel undeniably tender. The new awareness she had gained of her body amazed her. She hadn't expected that.

But then there was so much she hadn't expected.

She'd had the usual conversations with girlfriends, read the usual books, occasionally glanced at the usual articles in the women's magazines. She'd assumed that she *knew*.

She hadn't, not by a long shot. The plain fact was that she hadn't had a clue. Not that she made the mistake now of thinking that there was anything ordinary about what had happened between them. Tad was obviously an incredible lover. Her lover.

She savored that thought. It was so astounding, so unbelievable, yet true. This proud, determined, gorgeous man was her lover. As she was his.

She hugged her wonder to herself and glanced at him again. Exactly how long was he likely to sleep?

No, she wouldn't think like that. He was bound to need his rest. She would be patient, understanding, calmly cool. Whenever he woke up was fine with her. Nor would she necessarily assume that they would make love again. They might just talk.

Right.

Her eyes drifted past the thick column of his neck to his shoulders and beyond. She had seen fantastic-looking men before, mostly in photographs or the movies, to be sure, because the average everyday guy just didn't look like this. But being so close was another story, especially when she knew the touch and scent of his magnificent body, knew how it felt joined intimately with her own.

A tiny shiver ran through her.

Hardly aware of what she was doing, she reached

out a hand and lightly touched the curve of his right shoulder. He was so perfectly formed, so beautiful.....

Her hand drifted across his massive chest, downward to one of the tiny male nipples. She circled it lightly, fascinated when it puckered. A dusting of dark hair spanned the distance between his nipples, arching in a narrowing line down his abdomen. His middle was washboard-hard without an ounce of flap, his arms thick with muscle, the veins clearly articulated. There was no softness about him except...

Holding her breath, she eased the sheet down over his lean hips. The line of dark hair flared out again at his groin. She gazed at him, too fascinated to do otherwise. As she watched, his manhood stirred.

Her eyes flew to his face but his were still closed, his breathing slow and regular. She let out a little sigh of relief and returned to her study of him. His thighs were as hard as the rest of him—*all* the rest, now, except for the soft sack between them. She longed to touch him there, to cup the weight of him in her palm and caress him gently, but her boldness was deserting her. He had to wake up eventually and she definitely didn't want to be caught doing what she was—

"Good morning." The voice was low, husky and amused. Lisa groaned. She also felt herself turn bright red. Hastily, she tried to move away and might have managed it if Tad's hand hadn't lashed out so quickly, closing with implacable strength around her wrist and drawing her back to him.

"What's the matter?" he asked. "Don't you believe in finishing what you've started?"

Her eyes widened. She watched, spellbound, as he drew her hand to that part of him that had held her attention and laid her fingers gently against him.

Helpless, unable to deny her own desires, she began to stroke him. He was velvety smooth, hot, and oh, so tempting. Fascination held her spellbound. She barely noticed that he had let go of her. His hands were fastened on the sheet at either side of him, his features tautly drawn, his eyes glittering as together they watched what she did to him.

He bore it as long as he could, which actually wasn't very long at all. With a low groan, he reached for her.

"Sweet witch," he murmured as he lifted her above him, his mouth closing on her nipple at the same time that his hand found the soft flesh between her legs. She was already aroused; it needed only the smallest touch to open her fully for him. Holding her hips, he lowered her onto his hardness.

Lisa's back arched. She couldn't believe the sensations ricocheting through her. She moaned his name and moved, tentatively, experimentally.

"That's it, babe," he whispered and let her set the pace until his control finally broke and he thrust into her with a savage power that shattered them both.

A very long time later, Lisa felt herself being lifted. Her head rested on Tad's shoulder. He was carrying her.

She heard a rush of water as she was gently lowered into the whirlpool. He followed. The warm, soothing bath felt incredibly good. She moaned softly, nestling closer to him. He held her with infinite tenderness, murmuring to her softly, his big hands stroking her.

He'd left the lights off in the bathroom, but lit several candles. They sent flickering shadows across the marble pool. After a time, he took the heather-scented soap and gently washed her. He started with her back, turning her so that she was nestled between his legs, facing away from him.

Slowly, thoroughly, he ran his hands over her, reaching around to cup her breasts, lazily stroking the nipples with his soapy thumbs, moving lower over her belly. Being held and touched like that, unable to see him or touch him in turn, made her feel incredibly vulnerable.

She gasped, trying to twist away from him, but he held her firm, shifting her at last so that she was facing him. With a smile, he pressed her back against the opposite edge of the bath. Her long legs stretched out between them, pale and slim beneath the swirling water.

He began with her feet, massaging them lightly, moving up her calves with particular attention to the sensitive backs of her knees, and continuing on to the outsides of her thighs, his hands drifting ever closer

to the sensitive inner flesh. Her eyes closed as he
found her, touching her lightly again and again, keeping her in a heightened state of arousal just bordering
on release.

Long moments passed before she realized that he
had no intention of going further. Her eyes opened,
staring directly at him. He was watching her, smiling
with arrogant pleasure.

That was too much to bear. She drew her legs together and sat up suddenly. Her breasts bopped gently
as she took the soap from him. Her gaze locked on
his, she rubbed it between her hands, working up a
lather before splaying her fingers across his chest and
slowly moving them lower.

As she discovered what darkness and water had
concealed, her eyes widened. "I didn't think men
could…"

He grinned. "You honestly think I can be here like
this with you, touching you as I have, being touched,
and not become aroused?"

She flushed, knowing her ignorance was showing
but not caring all *that* much. "But we've already…"

His smile faded. Very gently, he drew her to him.
"I don't have to be inside you, babe. I understand it
might be too much, too soon. There are other ways."

Which she thought might be delightful to explore
at another time. But just then she knew exactly what
she wanted. Her breath warm in his ear, she told him.

Later still, he lifted her from the water and gently
dried her. The touch of the bath sheet against her

highly sensitized skin drew a moan from her. He persisted all the same, paying particular attention to her breasts and the cleft between her thighs. When the last droplets of water were gone, he lifted her again. She thought he meant to carry her back to bed but instead he laid her on the carpeted floor, turning her over onto her stomach.

"Stay there," he said and left her briefly.

She lay facedown, her arms stretched out at her sides and her legs open. The air was warm, or perhaps it was just that she felt so blazing hot. She stirred restlessly, self-consciousness stabbing through her, and was about to rise when his hand against the small of her back pushed her down again.

"Let me." He said nothing else, only lowered himself over her so that he was straddling her thighs. She felt him against her buttocks, felt his hands as they settled on her shoulders.

Felt something cool and slick...

And smelled heather.

Tad massaged her with long, slow strokes, his fingers kneading deeply. He began at the nape of her neck, working it strongly. Slowly, methodically, he made his way along each of her arms, down her back, pressing deeply to relieve the tensest muscles, over her derriere to her thighs and beyond. He caressed each separate finger and toe, every indentation and curve, returning unerringly again and again to those places that most needed his touch.

Except where the effect would have been greatest.

That he avoided, coming within inches but never quite touching her where she most yearned for him.

Lisa didn't know whether to laugh or curse. Surely she couldn't possibly become aroused again. She was too weak to walk, too deliciously replete to stir at all. There had to be a limit to what she could be made to feel...didn't there?

No, perhaps not.

When he finally turned her over, her nipples were pebble hard and she could not stop the instinctive thrust of her hips. He smiled but said nothing. She watched, helpless, as he poured more of the heather-scented lotion into his palms. A low whimper broke from her as she realized that he was very far from done.

Chapter 12

Lisa opened her eyes slowly. The effort was almost too much. She blinked, let her lids fall and began sinking back into sleep. Until a corner of what was left of her brain—a very tiny corner, undoubtedly—registered that it was no longer dark.

It was light and—therefore—day.

As in workday. As in rise and shine. As in there's still a world out there and you're not excused from it.

She groaned. The sound brought her eyes wide-open for real. It was all too damn familiar. She had groaned way too much last night, and moaned, and gasped, and sighed, and screamed and—oh, yes, lest she forget—whimpered.

She groaned again in acute embarrassment. Tugging the pillow from under her, she slammed it down over her head and tried to burrow into the mattress. Maybe she could disappear.

She couldn't face him. She absolutely couldn't. Not that she was ashamed or regretful or anything like that. She was just so incredibly...sensitive. Every nerve ending she possessed was alive and kicking. She felt swollen and tender in places she'd never much thought about before. And her brain—that pitiful thing again—had apparently decided this was a good time to play reruns of everything that had happened. Everything he'd done to her, everything she'd done to him, everything they'd done to each other, over and over and over...

The mattress muffled what would otherwise have been an extremely unladylike curse.

Unladylike? Ha! She'd passed unladylike sometime in the first two minutes last night, breezing straight by it on her high-stepping trip to Wantonville.

She had, hadn't she?

A languid smile curved her mouth as a certain pardonable self-satisfaction pushed out everything else. For a slow starter, she sure had closed the distance in one hell of a hurry.

With that thought to buoy her, she came out from under the pillow and took a cautious look around. The bedroom was empty and there were no sounds coming from the rest of the cottage.

She was alone, yet not alone. For there on the pillow beside her, the same pillow that still bore the imprint of Tad's head, was a freshly plucked wild rose.

And a note that said, "Sorry, we're out of heather."

She was smiling like a fool as she got out of bed and padded into the kitchenette to put the rose in water. There on the counter was a freshly brewed pot of coffee.

Now, roses were one thing, but a man who got up first and made the coffee...

Absolute heaven.

Cup in hand, she went into the bathroom where she resolutely refused to look in the direction of the whirlpool. A long shower later, she dressed in a simple cotton skirt and top, and left the cottage.

The really remarkable thing was that the world appeared unchanged. She shook her head, marveling over the obliviousness of nature, and strolled down the path to the main building. It was late enough that everyone else had finished breakfast and retreated to their offices. Later they would all reemerge, but for the moment she could slip in unseen.

She did just that, wondering if Tad was in his office, or at the house with Natalie. Thinking of the little girl reminded her of how little she really knew about him. He was obviously a far more complex man than his adoring fans had ever realized. Judging by what she'd heard the other night on TV, his business associates were just discovering that, as well. Equally obviously, he was devoted to saving rare places on earth through highly judicious and limited use, and he was particularly committed to Teal River.

He also knew women; really knew them in a way that she suspected most men would never even glimpse.

And women knew him, or at least sensed how he would be with them. No wonder so many had vied for his attention.

Oh, great. Just what she needed, a real downer of a thought. She'd been doing so well—happy, content, certain she'd done the right thing. Where had that particular piece of torment come from?

From wherever it was she had temporarily stashed her common sense.

Okay, reality-check time.

She angled her legs off the worktable, planted both feet firmly on the floor, and took a deep breath. Tad was an incredibly handsome and compelling man. Check. He also happened to be wealthy, powerful and a celebrity. Check. He could have virtually any woman in the world. Check, only virtue had nothing to do with it.

The woman he wanted was Lisa Preston.

Hold the check.

He *had* wanted her. She would have to be an absolute loony not to acknowledge that. But that was then and this was now.

He'd left the flower, he'd made coffee.

Gestures. Very nice gestures that just maybe weren't getting their first walk around the block.

She shook her head in self-disgust. It wasn't like her to be so massively insecure. A little uncertain now and then—who wasn't? But she'd grown up with great parents, loving brothers and a perfectly adequate sense of self-esteem. It wasn't like her to question her own worth.

Of course, not a whole lot she'd done in the last few days was like her, either.

She shook her head resolutely. No way she did this to herself. Work had always proved to be a reliable distraction in the past and she was sure it would now.

An hour later, that certainty was gone. All she'd managed to accomplish was several sketches of Tad. She'd never done much in the way of portraiture since she'd always preferred to concentrate on the graphic arts. But these weren't half-bad. They captured his strength and tenderness, the slant of his eyes when he looked at her in a particular way, the lean power of his body.

She sighed and stuck the sketchbook away in a drawer. This was ridiculous. What was it she'd said to him—"I am not a groupie"? It was time she remembered that.

The copy she had started work on the previous day needed editing. She opened the file, read it over, and started making changes. Some time later, she realized with a sense of relief that she actually had been able to concentrate. That made her feel as though she hadn't completely misplaced herself. She was still the same person she'd been yesterday—only different.

And hungry.

Oh, boy, was she hungry.

The person she used to be would have remembered to eat. Disgruntled, she went out into the common room to see what she could find. God bless whoever kept the food coming. She helped herself to a bowl of fish chowder and several slices of fresh-baked sourdough bread. On second thought, the yummy custard flan looked good, too. So did a couple of plums and—

"Looks like you could use a hand," Tad said.

Lisa turned suddenly, almost upsetting her tray. He was standing right behind her, having appeared with no warning whatsoever. Her hands shook. The tray teetered dangerously. He took it from her and stood holding it patiently while she stared at him.

No man, absolutely no man, had the right to look that good. Especially not after the night they'd put in. His ebony hair was pulled back in a queue at the nape of his neck, casting his chiseled features into hard relief. His eyes were well hidden behind those absurdly long lashes. And his mouth...

Forget his mouth. She absolutely was not going to think about that.

"Mind grabbing a sandwich for me?" he asked.

She shook her head and tried to convince herself nothing was rattling.

"What kind?"

He shrugged. "Whatever."

They moved over to a table near the windows. Lisa

had a cowardly impulse to retreat back to her office but before she could make a move in that direction, Tad had pulled out a chair for her. She sat facing him. Her appetite was gone. She couldn't think of anything but him, want anything but him, respond to anything but him.

The tip of her tongue moistened her lips nervously.

"Don't do that," he said.

She started, surprised. "Do what?"

"Use your tongue like that."

The muscles in her abdomen clenched. It was all she could do to keep her back from arching against the chair.

This was insane. They were in a public place. They hadn't even touched. How could she possibly become so aroused so fast?

She took a deep, shuddering breath and prayed for calm. She couldn't let him do this to her, she couldn't do it to herself. She had too much pride.

"How's Natalie?" she asked, grabbing for the one thing she thought might distract them.

He smiled, a warm, full, genuine smile that made her toes curl—literally. Great, now her shoes hurt.

"She's fine. She's gone to play with some friends."

"She's a great kid."

He nodded, took a bite of his sandwich. She watched helplessly as he chewed and swallowed. This must be what obsession was like, riveted to every tiny detail, a puppet responding to every little tug on the strings.

"We're going to the movies tomorrow. Want to come?"

He threw that out almost casually but she wasn't fooled. He was watching her too carefully. A tiny blossom of happiness unfurled in her. If she could only believe that there was something for them that he hadn't already shared with so many other women.

"Sure," she said, and discovered she was hungry after all.

Lisa worked late into the evening. She felt a need to make up for lost time but even more than that, she didn't want to think about the coming night. Tad had said nothing about it and she hadn't felt able to bring up the subject herself.

Now she regretted that she hadn't, but it was too late. They'd gone their separate ways after lunch; she hadn't seen him since.

It was well after sundown before she left the main building, and even then she didn't go to her cottage. Instead, she went for a walk, a long walk that she half hoped would drain off some of the nervous energy she felt.

The peace and tranquillity of the setting couldn't fail to soothe her somewhat but she still felt far from ready to sleep when she finally walked up the steps to the porch and opened the door.

The cottage was just as she'd left it. Tad's rose was

in a vase on the table. She stared at it for a long moment, feeling hollow inside. Why hadn't he said anything?

With a sigh, she loosened her hair from the ponytail she'd been wearing and let it fall over her shoulders. After the long walk—and the long day—a shower was just what she needed. Unbuttoning her blouse, she walked into the shadowed bedroom.

Looking out the window absently, she took the blouse off and draped it over the back of a chair. Her skirt was next. She stepped out of it automatically, kicking her shoes off at the same time. The weather had been too warm for panty hose. She wasn't wearing anything else except a lacy bra and matching panties.

Thinking about Tad, wondering what he was doing, she unsnapped the bra and let it slide off her shoulders. Catching it with a finger, she added it to the pile on the chair.

Soft air caressed her almost-nude body. She stretched her arms above her head, and groaned as she felt muscles that were not entirely recovered from the excesses of the previous night.

Flushing at the reminder of that, she hooked her thumbs under the elastic of her panties and eased them down her long legs. Completely nude, she turned toward the bathroom.

"What the hell took you so long?"

Lisa shrieked. She whirled toward the bed, the

source of that low, growling male voice. Even before her eyes focused on it, she knew what she would see.

Tad was stretched out on top of the covers. He was dressed in the jeans and shirt he'd worn earlier. His arms were folded behind his head. He was grinning.

Lisa had the absurd desire to cover herself—absurd because he'd already seen and touched every inch of her body. All the same, she had never felt so incredibly exposed...or so vulnerable.

She took a quick step back and demanded, "What are you doing here?"

His smile deepened. "Watching you strip. I liked it."

It really was possible to blush from the tips of the toes clear to the top of the head; Lisa was doing it. Obeying the impulse she could no longer deny, she crossed her arms over her breasts and took another step back.

"I...don't know if I like this...."

His eyebrows rose. He came off the bed in a smooth motion and walked toward her, tall, lithe, powerful, so virile that her heart hammered helplessly against the cage of her ribs.

She kept backing up, he kept coming. A shiver ran through her. She had the sudden, piercing knowledge of what it was to be hunted.

Without warning, her retreat was cut off by the wall between the bedroom and bath. She began to tremble and couldn't help herself. Holding up a hand in entreaty, she murmured, "Stop."

He stopped. The instant she said it, he stopped dead. Looking at her, he said very gently, "It's all right, Lisa. We're not going to do anything you don't want to do."

She stared at him, trying to gauge if he meant what he said. Tad didn't move. He gave her as long as she needed. Slowly, her fear eased and a very different emotion took its place.

This was the man who had made love to her last night with such extraordinary care and passion. Never once had he done anything to hurt her. Instead, he had wakened her to a glorious new knowledge of her own capacity for pleasure, both giving and receiving it.

She had trusted him through all those tumultuous hours. Surely, she could trust him now.

Her hands fell away from her breasts. Completely open to his gaze, she pushed herself away from the wall and took a tentative step toward him.

Still, he didn't move. He waited, fists clenched at his sides, while she came to him. The proud tilt of her head sparked his admiration but it was the gentle sway of her hips that sent lust stabbing through him so hard that it was all he could do not to howl. All the same, not until she was close enough for her breasts to rub lightly against his shirt did he finally respond.

Carefully, giving her time to object, he pressed her back against the wall. With his hand closed around both her wrists, he raised her arms over her head and held them there. His powerful thighs keeping her lower body in place, he used his free hand to stroke her.

The callused palm moved possessively from her slender throat, down over her full breasts and narrow waist to the swell of her hips and the cluster of silken curls between her legs. Again and again, he caressed her, accustoming her to his touch at the same time that he asserted his right to handle her as he chose.

"You're so beautiful," he murmured as he rolled a peaked nipple between his fingers, pinching lightly. "So exquisitely sensual." His mouth followed where his fingers had been as his hand slipped between her legs.

A sob broke from Lisa. She was much too far gone for any slow arousal. All day she had yearned for him, ached for him, and now he was there, holding and touching her, filling her with intolerable longing. She couldn't bear it.

"Please," she whispered helplessly, "I need you now."

He hesitated only long enough to look deeply into her eyes. What he saw there must have convinced him. He gave a low, guttural cry and raised both her legs, lifting them over his hips.

Her shoulders and upper back were pressed against the wall, her buttocks held in place against him by a rock-hard arm. He freed himself and she felt the hot urgency of his passion against her most sensitive flesh.

"I need you, too," he said harshly and thrust into her.

Time stopped. The world ceased to exist. There was nothing except the two of them, a man and a woman shorn of all pretense, locked together in the primal ritual of mating. Tad chanted her name, arching against her, licking and sucking her nipples, his thrusts steadily deeper and wilder, hammering into her.

Lisa met him fully. Her hands clawed at his back through the shirt. Her hips writhed. Scant moments passed before she was convulsed by spasms of pleasure so intense that she screamed.

When she was next aware, they were in the bathroom. Tad had turned the shower on. He was stripping off his clothes with one hand. The other kept hold of her.

"This *is* where you were headed, wasn't it?" he asked when he saw her surprise.

She couldn't do more than nod. Naked, he stood her under the water and stepped in beside her. If she had thought that the previous night's episode in the whirlpool was sensual excess, she was about to learn more of what that truly meant. By the time Tad flicked the shower off, she was absolutely limp.

He chuckled softly as he carried her back to the bed, yanked the covers open and slid her between them. The sheets were cool. She shivered but he was there instantly, gathering her close against him, warming her with the heat of his big, hard body.

"Go to sleep, sweetheart," he murmured and touched his lips to hers in a gesture so tender it sent a single silvery tear slipping down her cheek.

Tad watched that tear until he couldn't bear it any longer. Then he caught it on the tip of his finger, breathing silent thanks that no more followed. Lisa was asleep. He was grateful for that, too, because it gave him a chance to think.

Think? What was that? Oh, yeah, that thing he'd been meaning to do ever since—when was it?—ten days or so ago in the hotel.

Think. If he remembered correctly, that particular activity required the use of his brain rather than the other part of his body that had been calling all the shots of late.

A self-deprecating smile tightened his mouth. He was being a real bastard and he knew it. Lisa didn't, but then she was as innocent as a spring morning. The fear of what she would do when she figured it out gnawed at him, but not enough to change his mind.

It still stunned him that she'd been a virgin as recently as yesterday. That was one thing he definitely wasn't going to let himself think about very much. It just made what he was doing all the worse.

He'd never known a woman like her. Never even come close. She was beautiful, smart, talented, warm, kind and honorable. Nothing in his considerable experience had prepared him to deal with that. Self-indulgent, manipulative, selfish and uncaring, he could handle in a walk. But not Lisa. He had absolutely no idea how to bind her to him. And he was very determined to do that. *Very* determined.

No idea, that is, other than sex—hot, hard, intense, frequent, mind-blowing sex. The kind that she had no defenses against, that left her too stunned and replete to have any doubts, ask any questions, or—absolute worst case—decide they didn't belong together.

So that was what he was using. He knew he was shamelessly exploiting her innocence and her trust, and he went right ahead and did it anyway. But then that had been the case plenty in his life, hadn't it?

Anger at himself kept him awake long after the satiation of his body should have let him sleep. He lay holding her, stroking her shoulders and back, listening to the soft sound of her breathing.

And there, in the darkest hours of the night, he firmly put his guilt aside. He knew it wasn't fair or just—and it certainly wasn't politically correct—but Lisa Preston belonged to him. She had given him her virginity, her body and her trust. He would do anything he had to in order to keep her his.

Anything at all.

Chapter 13

There was a meeting the next day to discuss progress on Teal River. Everyone gathered in the common room, grabbing cups of coffee or tea, settling down comfortably. Lisa came in before Tad. They had parted shortly after dawn, he leaving her cottage somewhat later than he'd intended. She smiled at the memory.

Waking to what was supposed to be a "See you later" kiss had been very nice indeed. Especially when it had turned into so much more.

She added lemon to her tea and looked around to find a seat. The center of the common room was taken up by couches and armchairs grouped near a huge stone fireplace that was cold at the moment. All the same, the setting was warm and cheerful. It didn't look much like any business meeting she'd ever attended, but she wasn't surprised. Teal River was about as far from a typical business as it was possible to get.

Thinking about that, she sat down and sipped her tea. Looking around at the other people gathered there, she realized that a stranger suddenly coming upon them wouldn't have been able to figure out who was who. There was nothing to designate any sort of rank or pecking order. Everyone was an equal member of the team, equally valued and respected.

It was what some psychologists and sociologists called a nonhierarchical power structure, and it was generally considered to be very female. Males were supposed to thrive on the competition engendered by struggles for leadership and dominance. They needed to sort themselves out—the macho alpha types at the top and everyone else below.

Every company she'd ever worked for had functioned that way, no matter what kind of lip service was paid to the management strategy of the month. That kind of structure was so all-pervasive that women in the business world had no choice but to participate in it right along with the men, or get chewed up and spat out.

But not here. Teal River—owned by the most unrelentingly masculine man Lisa could ever have imagined—had a female power structure.

She almost laughed at the realization. Only a supremely confident man would ever have let such a

thing develop. But Tad had done more; he actively
encouraged and nurtured it. She wondered if it was
conscious on his part or if it just felt right to him.
Either way, he amazed her.

In so very many ways.

Oh, no, she wasn't going there. She absolutely
would not sit in a business meeting surrounded by
other people and allow herself to think about what
she and Tad had shared. If she had an ounce of self-
discipline left—and admittedly that was a big if—she
would use it to avoid that.

She did but only just. It was a very near thing,
made all the worse by Tad's arrival. He came in quietly, pausing to speak to several people, got himself
a cup of coffee and took a seat. He didn't so much
as glance at her.

That hurt, until she realized that he just might have
the same problem she did. At least, she hoped that
was the case. Otherwise, she was going to have to
find a very creative way to get back at him for ignoring her.

He continued to do so throughout the meeting until
it was her turn to speak. She gave a brief update on
promotion plans for Teal River, brief because she was
only just on the job and she knew no one would expect more.

People supported each other, offering help, sugges-
tions and praise. The chief architect and the head of
landscaping were already planning to get together
later to go over a few things. The environmentalist,

who more than anyone else seemed to have the final say on everything, was complimenting the waste-disposal specialist on the solution she'd come up with for recycling what were politely referred to as "organics" for use as fertilizer. Without exception, the staff was relaxed, cheerful and confident.

Would that she felt the same. She had every reason to do so, for truth be told, her work was going amazingly well. She couldn't have explained it if she'd had to but she simply knew how to promote Teal River.

Not in specifics, not completely and not yet. But she had the feel of the place and what it could evoke in people, the flow of emotion that would speak to the most fundamental desires for beauty and peace, and make the fulfillment of those desires irresistible.

She knew from experience that once she had the true sense of a project, everything else would follow smoothly. That she'd already achieved it in this case was remarkable but she didn't question why. She knew exactly what was responsible.

Or more correctly, who.

Several people had comments, all helpful and encouraging. But Tad said nothing. As before, he didn't even look at her. She wished she could be as controlled. Despite her best resolve, her eyes kept drifting to him. She loved the sound of his voice—calm, assured, sometimes serious, sometimes lightly humorous. So very different from the way he sounded in the throes of passion.

He looked...relaxed. Yes, that was it. He looked

very much at ease, focused on the task at hand, completely assured. She couldn't help but resent that.

It was all she could do to pay attention to what was being said. Unwillingly, she shifted in her seat, trying to find a more comfortable position. There wasn't one.

He glanced toward her just then. For a moment, his eyes narrowed. She stilled instantly, desperate not to draw his attention. She couldn't bear it if he continued to look at her. When he turned away, she breathed an almost-audible sigh of relief.

The meeting ended an hour or so later. Lisa got up quickly and went back to her office. Alone, she was able to relax, at least a little. But that didn't last long. She hadn't been there more than a few minutes when her phone rang. It startled her; she hadn't noticed it before.

"Hello...?"

"Are you all right?"

No preliminaries, just that hard question and the impatient wait for an answer.

Her hand tightened on the receiver. "Yes, of course."

He was silent for a moment. Softly, he said, "You looked as though you might be having some discomfort."

In all her life, Lisa couldn't remember blushing before she'd met Tad. She supposed she might have once or twice, but it hadn't made much impression on her.

Until now. *To the roots of her hair.* Wasn't that the expression? She finally understood what it meant. Her scalp actually quivered.

"No, I'm fine."

"You're sure?"

This was an absurd conversation to be having, especially by phone. She wouldn't continue it. "What do you want?"

Silence again. It lasted just long enough for her to consider how very foolish that question was. Could a blush become permanent?

"We're going to the movies. Remember?"

She all but sagged with relief. "The movies...you and Natalie...and me."

His laughter was low and intimate. "And Disney. Pick you up in half an hour. Okay?"

"Yes, sure, whatever. Half an hour."

She set the receiver down slowly. Her skin felt uncomfortably hot and now that he'd mentioned it—damn him—she was experiencing some discomfort. Not the kind he'd been concerned about, just the kind he caused.

But she would get over it. She smiled at the thought of seeing Natalie again. She loved kids, adoring her nieces and nephews, and looked forward to having her own someday. Unbidden, an image rose of herself swollen with child and Tad smiling at her as he gently, sinuously caressed her ripe belly, his mouth lowering to her breasts, heavy with milk.

The force of that was so powerful that she moaned.

When she felt able to, she went to the ladies' room and splashed cold water on her face and wrists. It helped a little. Running a brush through her hair, she stared at herself in the mirror.

How could she possibly not look any different. *How?* She was *not* the person she'd been a few days ago, no matter how desperately she tried to convince herself. If she never saw Tad again—and the thought was like a red-hot brand inside her—he would touch her to the very end of her days.

Upon closer examination, she had to admit that she was pale. Even her eyes had lightened, the shards of gold standing out starkly while the normally more mundane brown appeared to be in retreat. Only her mouth looked full and ripe, naturally shaded a dark rose, made all the more distinct because her lips were still slightly swollen.

Wishing she'd bothered with makeup, she straightened her clothes and went back outside. A car had pulled up in front of the main building. She recognized a top-of-the-line four-wheel-drive vehicle that made her own transportation look like a tin can.

Tad was at the wheel. Natalie was in the back, securely fastened into a booster seat, the kind that served as a transition out of car seats. She was familiar with them only because her brothers and their wives had used them. From what she'd seen elsewhere, most people didn't bother.

But Tad did. He was very protective of his little daughter.

Natalie waved a hand and smiled. Lisa did a quick double take. Her smile was exactly like Tad's. In that, at least, they might have been cloned. Yet he'd said he didn't know whether he'd actually fathered her and he'd made it clear he didn't care. Whether he had or not, he certainly was her father now in every way that mattered.

"Hi," Natalie said. "Daddy said you're coming with us."

"That's right," Lisa replied as she slid into the passenger seat. "I hope you don't mind."

Natalie frowned. She glanced at her father who said nothing, merely waited. With a little shrug, she said, "Why would I mind?"

Lisa didn't have an answer for that. How could she begin to explain to the pixie that some children wouldn't like sharing their father with anyone? Natalie was obviously too openhearted—and too secure—to ever have such a possibility occur to her.

"No reason," Lisa said. Returning the little girl's smile, she said, "I'll share my popcorn."

"Buttered?" Natalie asked.

Solemnly, Lisa agreed.

A small hand reached out from beside Lisa, fumbled in the popcorn container she held and withdrew a buttery fistful. Natalie munched without ever taking her eyes from the screen. Neither did Lisa. They were both completely caught up in the movie, Lisa every bit as carried away as Natalie.

Watching them, Tad grinned. The "girls" were having a great time. As for himself...he was willing to admit that the producers had a knack for making movies that delighted children without making the adults cringe.

The music was the best part. He resigned himself to buying yet another cassette and playing it yet another kazillion times. Not to mention the required assortment of other merchandise.

At least the flying-carpet thing was over. For a while, Natalie had insisted that every carpet in the house was capable of aerial transportation. He'd held his breath more than a few times when he thought she just might try going off a balcony on a throw rug.

They were headed into the big finale. The music soared, lots of strings and trumpets with kettledrums in the background. It had a fine, majestic sound. The kids—of all ages—in the audience were eating it up. There were only a handful of adults that he could glimpse who appeared to be just benignly getting through it.

As the credits rolled and the houselights came up, they stood. Natalie was chattering about how great it had been and Lisa was right there with her, comparing notes.

Tad was struck by how easy they were with each other. There was nothing stilted or artificial about the way they interacted. That was a relief to him. It helped ease the guilt he'd been feeling for keeping his daughter in what was really a very artificial environment.

Except for the nanny and his own mother, Natalie had very little contact with women. She knew the mothers of her small circle of friends, but only superficially. Later in the year, when she started prekindergarten she would have a teacher—almost certainly female—and she would get to know her better.

But Natalie had never even met the women who flitted through her father's life, much less had anything to do with them. He'd made damn sure of that.

Until Lisa.

He'd had no hesitation at all about putting the two of them together. It had seemed completely natural, and now that he could see it in reality, he knew he'd been right.

Lisa didn't especially relate to Natalie as a child—at least not in the empty-headed, saccharine-voiced way people tended to treat kids. Instead, she spoke to her with enjoyment and respect, and she got exactly the same in return.

They were completely relaxed with each other, chattering on about the movie as they left the theater and walked the short distance to the pizza parlor that was Natalie's favorite after-movie treat.

The town, about twenty miles west of Teal River, was small but fully functional. It had all the essentials—from a decent bar to a coin-operated Laundromat, video rental store, better-than-average mechanic, and no fewer than six places to eat that wouldn't kill you. It reminded Tad of some of the towns in Arizona, where he'd grown up.

At this hour, there were a good number of people out on the street, some coming from the movie, others drifting in for the next show or otherwise going about their business. There were a few stray looks in his direction but apart from that, nobody paid them any attention.

Tad really appreciated that. The first few times he'd come into town, people had glanced his way but nobody had said anything to him. Word had already spread that he was buying Teal River and people had come to whatever conclusions they wanted about that.

However they'd felt about it, they respected his privacy. They let him lead a normal life, taking his daughter to the movies, going out for a bite to eat. In that, they gave him a gift rarer and more precious than they could have known.

The pizza parlor was crowded with families—kids in high chairs banging spoons on their trays, the older ones chowing down, everybody talking at once, moms and dads wiping mouths, dabbing up spilled drinks, generally keeping order. The waitresses were unflappable; they had serenity down to a science.

They got a table near the counter, opposite the big-screen television that was another draw for the place. Not for Natalie, though. She ignored it in favor of watching the pizza men who weren't averse to putting on a little show for a kid.

"Very impressive," Lisa said as one particularly

agile wheel of dough rose almost to the ceiling. "Did you ever try to do that?" she asked Tad.

"Uh, no, can't say I have."

"I did. It came down right on my head. I was still finding gooey bits of flour in odd places the next day."

A waitress came over and took their order. She gave Lisa a single, registering sort of glance but there was nothing unfriendly or intrusive about it; just the kind of look someone new to a place would get. When the woman was gone, Lisa leaned across Natalie and asked, "Did I pass?"

"Must have," Tad said. "She didn't dump any pizza on your head."

"It's early yet."

For a child who had just put away the better part of a supersize serving of popcorn, Natalie had an amazing appetite. She got her own pizza with everything, which in her case included mushrooms, onions, two kinds of peppers, sausage and—this part made Lisa flinch—pineapple. The grown-ups contented themselves with a second, more modest pie that gave a digestive system the chance to survive to another day.

Lisa stared at the little girl in wonder as she promptly devoured four slices. Finally, she had to ask, "Honey, would you mind telling me where you're putting all that?"

Natalie wiped her fingers clean on a paper napkin, cocked her small head to one side, and absolutely deadpan said, "Daddy says it goes straight to my hollow leg."

Tad laughed. "She's always been a big eater," he said. "Given her size, I admit it's kind of amazing."

It was a bit more than that. Lisa was genuinely impressed and she'd grown up in a family that thought having twin refrigerators was normal.

"My brothers have got to meet you," she told Natalie.

The little girl took a sip of her soda and set the cup down neatly. She looked from Lisa to her father and back again. Slowly, as though deciding something in her own mind, she nodded.

"I think I should have brothers." Just for good measure, she added, "And sisters, too, of course. Two of each would be nice."

The adults stared at each other across the table. Neither one of them said anything. Natalie observed them for a moment, then started on another slice of pizza.

Tad cleared his throat. He finally managed to take his eyes off Lisa and looked at his daughter. She had never said anything about wanting siblings. Never asked him about it nor even hinted that the subject had occurred to her. Apparently, she'd been saving it up.

He had a sudden piercing sense of what it would mean to be sitting someplace like this with several children instead of just one, not unlike many of the families around them. Granted, some of the parents looked harried and some of the kids were doing a good imitation of feeding time at the zoo. But overall he didn't think it would be too bad. Truth be told, he kind of liked the idea. A lot.

Just so long as Lisa was sitting right there with him. He would be scared to death of it otherwise.

His eyes crinkled with amusement at himself. What would she say if she knew what he was thinking? She would probably jump out of her skin. It was so soon for them—much too soon.

Natalie was watching the pizza man again. The guy was definitely an artist. He made that wheel of dough fly.

"Why does it get bigger when it spins?" Natalie asked.

Tad hesitated. Usually he could handle her questions, but this one had him stumped.

"Centrifugal force," Lisa supplied.

Father and daughter both looked at her.

She shrugged. "It's being drawn outward from the center. Things do that when they revolve. It has to do with motion and gravity."

"Like a spin picture?" Natalie asked.

Lisa nodded. "Those wheel things where you put a piece of paper down and squirt paint on it while it turns? Yep, same idea."

"How do you know stuff like that?" Tad asked.

"I have nieces and nephews. Talk to kids long enough, eventually you know everything." She thought for a moment, then said quite seriously,

"How about spin pizza? A big wheel, lots of batteries, and you get to squirt on your favorite toppings."

Natalie looked entranced by the idea. Also, very impressed. She regarded Lisa with definite respect.

Tad laughed. He felt so damn good. Life had taught him to be wary, to doubt everything and trust nothing. But he forgot about that now and didn't question what was happening. Maybe later, but not now.

It was getting late. For all her energy, Natalie was starting to flag. Tad got up to pay the check. When he turned around again, his eyes hit the big-screen TV.

It was tuned to one of those trash "news" programs that littered the airways. A guy with lacquered hair was moving his lips but Tad couldn't hear him. There was too much noise in the restaurant.

It didn't matter. Even as he watched, the video cut to a picture of himself standing next to Melanie George. They were in a small courtyard filled with flowering plants. He had no trouble recognizing the place, but then why would he, since he'd been there many times, most recently only a couple of days before?

Melanie had her hands braced on his chest. Her blond hair tumbled around her shoulders. Her face was lifted, her lips parted; she was smiling enticingly.

The photo preserved a modicum of decency but it was clear to even the most casual viewer that Melanie didn't happen to be wearing anything.

He tore his gaze away and stared at the table he'd

just left. Natalie had snuggled her head against Lisa. Her eyes were closed. His daughter wasn't seeing anything.

Lisa was a different story. She was staring right at the TV. Her pale face and dark, pained eyes said it all.

Chapter 14

"You can drop me off here," Lisa said. They were just nearing the main building, having entered the Teal River boundaries a few minutes before. Her hand was already on the door handle. She wasn't looking at Tad, but then she hadn't looked at him since the scene in the pizza parlor.

Natalie was in the back seat fast asleep. If she hadn't been, he could have argued with Lisa, refused to do what she asked, demanded that they talk.

But he couldn't do any of that, not with his daughter right there.

He could only murmur her name as she got out of the car, but either she didn't hear him or she chose to ignore it. Without a word or so much as a backward glance, she walked away.

He watched her go. Her head was held high and her back was very straight. She looked proud, defiant and absolutely determined.

His hands clenched on the steering wheel, the knuckles showing white. Anger washed over him. Who the hell did she think she was to walk away from him like that? Without giving him the smallest chance. She'd tried him, judged him, and now she'd delivered his sentence. Miss Lisa Preston had apparently decided he was dirt beneath her feet.

Damn her to hell and back. He'd come too far in his life—and done it the hard way—to let anyone treat him like that. At the very least, she was going to hear him out.

But first he had to take care of Natalie.

Miss Harris, that treasured gem of an extremely expensive English nanny, was waiting up. It was hardly late but even if it had been, she would have been there. Tad could dismiss her devotion to Natalie as properly bought and paid for, but he knew that wouldn't be fair.

He'd hired her when Natalie was six months old and finally able to do without professional nursing. The plump, gray-haired woman who earned more than many two-paycheck families had come with the highest possible recommendations. She'd deserved them.

"I'll take her, sir," she said quietly, easing Natalie from her father's arms. The little girl never stirred. Miss Harris smiled at her gently. "Pizza again, sir?"

Tad ran a hand through his hair and nodded. His thoughts were still too much on Lisa. "Just the usual. You know it doesn't do her any harm."

Miss Harris looked aghast at the very idea. "Oh, no, of course not, sir. You'd never allow Natalie to be harmed by anything."

That was true, he wouldn't. His protection of her was as absolute as he could possibly make it. In the back of his mind, he knew that he would have to lighten up on that as she got older but he would face any such decision at the last possible moment.

As for right now, he knew Natalie was as safe and well cared for as she possibly could be. Miss Harris carried her upstairs, leaving him alone.

He went into a room off the two-story entry hall. In an earlier era, it would have been referred to as a study. Nowadays, it was very much a home office. The desk was a slab of black marble resting on coiled steel legs. It was bare except for a state-of-the-art computer system he used to manage his far-flung business and investment interests. Nearby, a credenza held two large television sets, VCRs, and stereo equipment.

One entire wall was made up of windows looking out toward the river. Another wall held a wet bar. Tad went over to it. He opened a bottle of Scotch, poured himself two fingers and knocked the drink back hard.

It burned going down and sent a sudden rush of heat through his body. It fed the heat already there, anger mingling with arousal.

He closed his eyes for a moment and again saw Lisa walking away from him. His whole body tightened in rejection of that. It was what he had feared from the beginning, as soon as he'd realized how different she was and how at a loss he was to deal with her.

And now it was happening.

Or it would be if he didn't put a stop to it damn fast.

He eyed the Scotch, decided against it, and put the bottle away. The last thing he needed was encouragement. He was already so fueled by the combination of lust, pain and rage that he wasn't sure how much to trust himself. Deliberately, he waited until his breathing was steadier and he felt at least a little more in control.

Only then did he leave the house again.

Lisa forced herself to go through the motions of getting ready for bed. She took a shower, brushed her hair and put on a nightgown, but she was hardly aware of doing any of it. All she could think about was Tad—and Melanie.

There were any number of possible explanations. She knew that as surely as she knew that she should have talked with Tad. But she hurt so much and she'd been worried about Natalie, not wanting the child to realize anything had happened. All she could think of was getting away.

Standing in the kitchenette, she wrapped her arms

around herself and trembled. Tomorrow she would talk with him. She would ask him calmly about the photograph. It had probably been taken months ago, before he and Melanie broke up. She would apologize for flying off the handle. They might even laugh about it.

Tomorrow.

Feeling a little more settled and reassured, she was about to pour herself a glass of milk when her body froze. The silence of the night was punctured by a harsh banging on the cottage door.

She straightened slowly—everything seeming to slow down at that moment—and stared at the door as though she'd never seen it before. So powerful was the force of the blows it was receiving that the door trembled.

So did she as Tad's hard, remorseless voice washed over her. "Open up, Lisa. Right now!"

She didn't want to open that door. Oh, God, she really didn't. He was so angry. She couldn't entirely blame him—she'd behaved badly, but not enough for the rage she sensed clear through the barrier still separating them.

Tomorrow...

"Go away," she said and marveled at how she'd found the courage. She even sounded strong and determined. Incredible. "We can talk in the morning."

Nothing. No response at all except that the pounding on the door stopped. She was just breathing a tiny sigh of relief, thinking she'd made him see reason, when the door was kicked in so savagely that it almost came off the hinges.

Tad stepped through it. He stood—dark, powerful, implacable—with his legs planted firmly apart and his hands on his hips, and he glared at her.

"Just what the hell did you think you were doing?" he demanded.

Lisa opened her mouth to speak but nothing came out. Never in her wildest imagination—and it had gotten *very* wild of late—could she have anticipated such a scene. He'd known she hadn't wanted him near her and he hadn't cared. He had kicked the door in. That door—that locked door that was supposed to protect her—had barely slowed him down. His strength was such that no defense was likely to stand against him.

At that precise moment it occurred to her that she was completely unprepared to deal with a man in his state of mind. She knew nothing about violence. Her parents had never believed in spanking, had never so much as raised a hand to one of their children. Her brothers, though older, bigger and stronger than she, had always treated her gently.

The men she'd dated might not have stirred her passion, but they were decent men all the same. She'd seen and read about what happened elsewhere but never had she thought she would experience it. Now she was very much afraid she was about to.

Unless she did something *fast.*

Every instinct for self-preservation that she possessed was screaming at her to get away. Without hesitation, she turned and ran.

Tad followed right after her. There weren't many places she could go. The door of the bedroom wasn't going to hold him back, either, but she slammed it shut all the same, locked it and yanked a chair under the knob.

She dashed to the bedroom window and began opening it as wide as she could. The window was big enough for her to get out through. After that, she wasn't sure what she would do but she couldn't think about that now.

Her nails tore on the window sash. She moaned but didn't stop. Behind her the bedroom door met the same fate as the first.

Desperate, she dared a glance over her shoulder. Tad stood just inside the room. He was scowling, his face was slightly flushed and a jagged pulse beat in his jaw.

"Stop that," he ordered.

She ignored him and redoubled her efforts. Just another few inches... But the window was new, like most of the other buildings at Teal River, and it hadn't been opened so wide since leaving the factory. It gave but only grudgingly, and not in time.

His hand closed on her arm. Stark, raw fear roared through Lisa. She struggled frantically, pounding her fists against his chest as she tried to wrench herself free.

He cursed under his breath and grabbed her other

arm, dragging her away from the window. She kicked out at him and heard him curse again.

"Let me go!"

She was screaming, fighting him with every ounce of her strength, and it was having no effect at all, except seemingly to make him even angrier.

His rock-hard arm wrapped around her waist. He pulled her away from the window and toward the bed. "Stop it! Dammit, stop!"

She wasn't listening to him. Terror blocked out everything else. Drawing on lessons ingrained in her long ago by very protective brothers, she raised her knee and slammed him between the legs.

His shout of pain and rage roared through the room. She felt a stabbing regret at having hurt him, pushed it aside and tried to move away. She couldn't. Incredibly, despite being doubled over in agony, Tad still held on to her.

If her fear before had known no bounds, this was even worse. She had retaliated against him in the most effective way a woman could, and still he had control of her. As hurt as he was, he would recover and then—

Summoning all that was left of her strength, she made a final, desperate bid to get away. And she almost succeeded. For just a second, he was forced to let go.

Then his hand lashed out, closing on her thin cotton nightgown. There was a shrill, ripping sound as the garment was torn completely off her.

God, she was beautiful. Doubled over in pain that had to compete with the rage still clawing at him, Tad could still appreciate the perfection fully exposed to his gaze. Her body was slender but curved, softly rounded, lithe, exquisite. His gaze drifted from her high, firm breasts with the dusty pink areolas down over her slender rib cage and flat abdomen to the apex of her thighs concealed by soft curls.

Slowly he straightened. And slowly, too, the enormity of what had just happened began to sink into him.

She was terrified. Ever since he'd kicked down her door and forced his way into the cottage, she'd been in the grip of stark fear. How could she have been otherwise? He'd given her every reason to suspect— and expect—the worst.

Shame hit him harder than the blow she'd landed. Instinctively, he reached out to her, wanting only to give comfort. His hand stilled when she flinched and drew back. She was watching him with the wide eyes of a doe caught in the glare of headlights. Unable to move, she could only wait to discover what he would do next.

What was left of his anger died a cold, hard death. He still throbbed with pain but he no longer felt it. Nothing mattered except Lisa and what she was feeling.

"God, sweetheart, I'm sorry. I'd never hurt you." He held out his arms and breathed a silent prayer. If he had pushed her too far...

A small, hiccuping sob escaped her. She stared at him. He waited, not moving, just praying. *Please...*

Perhaps she saw something in his eyes. Or perhaps she was just the most generous woman on earth. She took one small, tentative step toward him. He didn't wait for anything more, but enfolded her in his embrace, holding her tightly as he murmured, "Shh, it's all right. I'm sorry, so sorry. Don't cry. Oh, God, please don't cry."

She did, but only a little, and she stopped as soon as he tilted her face back and kissed her. The kiss was tender, holding nothing of passion, intended only to soothe. It seemed to work for she relaxed slightly, her head nuzzling into his shoulder. She gave a soft, exhausted sigh.

He was going to have to find a proper way to give thanks for this. Maybe build a cathedral or something. In the meantime, he lifted her gently and carried her to the bed.

She clung to him, not letting go as he lowered her so that he remained stretched out beside her, holding her with great care. The blow she'd dealt him should have left him unmanned for some time yet, but apparently his body didn't understand that. Within minutes, her nudity and her nearness were having the predictable effect.

He groaned and didn't even realize it until she raised her head and looked at him. "What's wrong?"

"Aside from the fact that I'm a total bastard? Nothing, darling, nothing at all."

She didn't appear to believe him but at least she laid her head back down on his chest. He managed to grab a corner of the spread and lift it over her so that she was shielded at least from his gaze. That helped but not a whole lot.

After a while, when she had stopped trembling, he relaxed his hold on her. She stiffened as he moved to leave the bed but he reassured her with a gentle touch.

"I just want to take care of the door, babe. I'll be right back."

She blushed then and he saw that she was remembering what had happened. Quickly, not wanting to leave her alone any longer than he had to, Tad secured the front door. It wouldn't lock and the hinges were loose but at least it would afford them some privacy until he could get it fixed in the morning.

No, until he could fix it. He wasn't about to get anyone else to do it and invite all the questions that would be asked, if only silently.

He returned to the bedroom. Lisa lay with her eyes closed. Her face was very pale. The extreme emotion she had experienced had drained away all the accustomed vivacity of her nature. She was exhausted. They needed to talk but that would have to wait. In all conscience, he couldn't force anything else on her.

But he couldn't leave her, either. Silently, he stripped off his clothes and got into bed beside her. She made a small murmur as he gathered her to him but it was a sound of contentment, not protest.

Her forgiveness and her trust were the sweetest

balm he had ever known. He drew her closer, twining his legs with hers. He knew the exact moment when she slipped into sleep. Her body relaxed completely and her breath became slow and deep, the soft exhalations lightly ruffling the hair on his chest.

He lay on his back, holding her, and resigned himself to an extremely uncomfortable night.

At the very least, he deserved it.

A frantic cry yanked Tad from sleep. He sat up suddenly, aware of nothing—not where he was or why—except the sobs of the woman in his arms.

Lisa.

Pain that had nothing whatsoever to do with his earlier—and now forgotten—injury tore through him. He reached out to snap on the bedside lamp. By its soft glow, he could see her, still nestled against him, still asleep, yet with tears coursing down her cheeks.

Brokenly, she whispered, "N-no...don't..."

He couldn't stand it. Pulling her upright, he shook her lightly. "Lisa, wake up! God, wake up!"

She did, coming to consciousness as abruptly as he had done, and stared at him. "Wh-what...?"

He gave a low groan and pulled her back into his arms. Forcing himself to calm, he stroked her hair just as he would Natalie's when she had a nightmare. But this was no child he held. This was a beautiful, passionate woman whose fear he himself had caused. He had to find a way to make amends.

Slowly, the nature of his caress changed. His big

hand gentled her, stroking her petal-soft skin from neck to thigh. At the same time, his mouth carefully touched hers.

He was fully prepared to stop if she showed the slightest resistance or hesitation. But she did not. Her lips parted on a sigh of pleasure. A bolt of raw lust shot through him when the tip of her tongue touched his tentatively.

Calling on all his control, he eased her over so that he was above her. He kissed every inch of her face and throat, nibbling her earlobes, laving them with his tongue. Before he was done, she was holding on to him frantically.

He ignored the savage, demanding response of his body and continued down hers. Her nipples were pebble hard and glistening wet before he took his mouth from them. Gently, he nudged her thighs apart. His fingers grazed her again and again as her hips arched and she writhed, pleas breaking from her.

"I can't bear this.... It's too much.... End it...please!"

His mouth replaced his hand. He brought all his skill to bear, lifting her higher and higher, driving her to a completion so intense that she screamed. Even then, he held her tightly against him, refusing to let her come down even a little. Her second climax followed within moments of the first. It left her sobbing, not with fear as she had before, but with pleasure so intense as to be almost beyond endurance.

Her recovery was slow but with it came the full

awareness of what had happened—and what hadn't. Her eyes dark with bewilderment—and concern—she raised herself enough to look at him.

"Tad…you didn't… Are you…?" All the newly returned color fled from her cheeks.

His smile was grim. After everything that had happened, she was worried about him, fearing how much damage the blow she'd landed had actually done. He reached for her gently. "It's all right, sweetheart."

More puzzled than ever, she brushed her hand down him. He flinched when she touched his fullness. "I don't understand," she said softly.

"Tonight is for you," he said. "Only for you."

She was still trying to absorb that when he began to love her again.

Pancakes. Someone was making pancakes. And bacon.

Lisa flicked one eye open. She was lying on her stomach, arms and legs spread out in all directions. There was a sheet over her but it came no higher than her hips. She turned over slowly and sat up, drawing the covers with her.

The delectable aromas made her stomach growl. She started to get out of bed but froze suddenly, remembering.

Her cheeks flamed. Last night…

For one brief moment, she considered the possibility that she'd dreamed it all. Tad furiously angry, breaking the door down, herself so terrified and then...

Her body stirred with an entirely different kind of hunger. Memory flooded back. She trembled, her eyes glazing with remembered passion.

He had made love to her over and over, one climax flowing into the next until the rapturous, cresting pleasure seemed continual and endless.

He let her sleep when her mind and body could do nothing else, but only for brief periods and always to wake her with his hands and mouth bringing her to ecstasy yet again. And yet, never once had he entered her. Not once had he sought release for himself.

She put her fingers to her lips with a sound of dismay. Oh, God, she truly had hurt him. She remembered the hard fullness of him that had lulled her into believing he had recovered, but obviously he hadn't really.

What could she say to him? What could she do?

Quickly, she left the bed. Too anxious to look for clothes, she wrapped the sheet around her and went out to the kitchenette. At the first sight of Tad, she stopped cold.

He was standing at the stove with his back to her, wearing only a pair of jeans that fit him snugly. The broad, heavily muscled expanse of his back drew her gaze irresistibly. There was such power within him, such strength and will. She shivered to think of it.

She must also have made some sound, for he turned suddenly and saw her. The spatula he held added a sweetly ordinary touch to what otherwise would have been an almost unbearably tense moment.

With memories of the previous night still making her body tighten, Lisa could barely meet his eyes. When she did at last, she found him gazing at her with such tender care and concern as to steal her breath away.

Without hesitation, she went to him and laid a hand lightly on his chest.

He put the spatula down. He gathered her into his arms. He kissed her with sweet, gentle passion. Together, their bodies communicated in a way words would never have achieved, reaffirming their essential closeness.

Even when the kiss ended, Tad kept her against him, her head resting in the crook of his shoulder and his hand gently caressing her hair. Softly, he murmured, "I'm so sorry, sweetheart."

She remembered him saying that in the night, remembered the regret and remorse that had poured out of him. Tears came to her eyes. "I'm sorry, too. I never meant to hurt you."

He drew back a little and looked at her, puzzled. "What do you mean?"

Her cheeks flamed. It was absurd after all that had passed between them but she felt acutely self-conscious. Finally, she said, "When I...you know...my knee... I never realized it would be so...disabling...."

He stared at her a moment longer before his mouth

twitched in a smile. "Honey, I won't claim it didn't hurt like hell but it was over by the time I got into bed with you." Stroking her cheek with the back of his hand, he added, "You know that."

The husky, intimate timbre of his voice made the shivers that had started as soon as she woke deepen. He was close enough for her to feel him along her breasts, her belly, her thighs. Feel, too, that he was as aroused as she was.

"Then, why didn't you...?"

His hand settled at the small of her back, pressing lightly. "Come into you? Because it wasn't for me, it was for you, because of what I'd done.... I frightened you."

The full meaning of the previous night roared through her. He had deliberately denied himself, hour after hour, concentrating solely on pleasuring her with no thought to his own needs.

Innocent she might have been only a few days before, but she was still capable of realizing the nearly superhuman self-discipline that had required. And a depth of caring so profound as to seem to speak of...

She raised herself up slightly on her toes. Brushing his mouth with hers, she murmured, "I love..." Her lips teased, tantalized. Her hand holding the sheet opened.

The fabric slid down her, baring her breasts, her waist, catching for a moment at the curve of her hips until she shrugged it off to fall in a pool at her feet. Nipping, sucking, coaxing his mouth, she rubbed the tips of her breasts against his chest. "I love...cold pancakes. Don't you?"

He made a harsh, inarticulate sound and swooped her into his arms.

They skipped the pancakes. It was Saturday, and although the staff at Teal River worked all sorts of hours, nobody would be looking for them. Natalie had a friend's birthday party to attend, with a shopping expedition thrown in for good measure. She would be busy until evening.

Having come together twice in fiery and very mutual satisfaction, they slept, not awakening until almost noon. After a long—and highly enjoyable— shower together, Lisa busied herself making sandwiches while Tad repaired the doors.

He had to leave for just a few minutes to get the necessary tools. She was vividly aware how much she missed him during even that short time. When he returned, she insisted he eat first; then she cleaned up as he worked.

The silence between them was natural and companionable. She watched him out of the corner of her eye and couldn't help but be struck by his competency in performing a task that she wouldn't have known how to even begin.

As he finished the front door and crossed the room to the bedroom, she couldn't resist asking, "Are all men born knowing how to do things like this or do you get special training?"

He laughed and stopped long enough to wrap an arm around her waist, drawing her close for a quick kiss. "What do you think goes on at all those men-only meetings we have?"

"What men-only meetings?"

"Oops, I forgot. We're not supposed to tell."

She laughed and tried to swat him but that didn't go very far. The bedroom door stayed unrepaired until late afternoon. When Tad finally got around to it, Lisa lay on her side and watched.

There was something deliciously wicked about watching a stark-naked man perform such a mundane chore. She felt so relaxed, so at ease. It was difficult to believe how much had changed since the previous evening.

Thinking of that made her frown. They still hadn't talked. She wasn't sure that she wanted to but Tad had other ideas. When he'd finished with the door, he came over to the bed, sat down and looked at her very seriously.

"I have to tell you something."

She fought a horrible, cowardly impulse to cover her ears.

"I saw Melanie when I went to L.A. That photo must have been taken then." Grimly, he added, "Damn paparazzi have better equipment than the CIA."

"I see...."

"No, you don't, but I want you to. I stayed at a place I've used before. It's very private, or at least it's supposed to be. Melanie found out I was there and showed up. She followed me into the courtyard. When I told her there was no way we'd start up again, she pulled one of her usual impulsive stunts.''

"She...took off her clothes?"

He nodded. "Nobody can strip faster than Melanie. I think she has her outfits specially made for that.''

"And somebody was watching...taking photos." The thought made her skin crawl. She couldn't imagine being exposed like that.

"I wouldn't put it past her to have set the whole thing up. She'll do anything for publicity.''

Faintly, Lisa said, "It sounds to me that she was willing to do anything to get you back."

He shrugged. "Melanie's always been the one to walk out on a relationship, and she's had plenty of practice doing it. I gather she didn't like discovering what it was like on other side of the fence.''

Lisa considered that. Melanie George was easily one of the most beautiful women in the world. No doubt she was also a match for Tad in sexual experience. She'd stood right in front of him, naked, offering herself, and he'd turned her down.

He had, hadn't he?

She could simply ask. She almost did. But the look in his eyes stopped her.

He looked worried. Not guilty, or secretive, or even blandly innocent. Just worried. And he was watching her with such intentness that she could barely breathe.

She swallowed against the tightness in her throat. Her head lifted and she looked straight at him.

"Okay."

He frowned, not understanding. "Okay, what?"

"Okay, you've explained. I appreciate it, and I'm sorry I flew off the handle the way I did. I'll know better next time." Quickly she added, "Not that I think there will be a next time but if there is, which there won't be, but just in case..."

"You believe me." His face filled with wonder and something more—gratitude. Sweeping, profound gratitude.

Lisa's throat clogged with tears. Instinctively, she reached out to him, needing to comfort and reassure.

"I believe you," she affirmed, holding him, her hands stroking down his powerful back, her breath warm against his neck. "I believe you...I believe you—"

He caught her words with his mouth and lowered her back onto the bed.

Chapter 15

Natalie squealed with delight, kicked her small legs out, and dived under the water with all the agility of a baby seal. She surfaced several yards away to grin at the grown-ups.

"Daddy says I should have gills," she called to Lisa.

"Are you sure you don't?" Laughing, Lisa dived after the little girl and caught up with her quickly. "Let me see. I'll bet you do." She wiggled her fingers behind tiny ears, tickling.

Natalie's excited laughter prompted her father's. He cut through the water with hardly a ripple, coming up right next to them. "If we're determining who's ticklish…" he said with a grin and reached for Lisa.

"Oh, no!" she yelped and fled but not fast enough.

He caught her ankle, pulled her to him and waggled his fingers in front of her nose. That was enough. She started laughing helplessly but she wasn't about to give up. Without warning, she reached out and tickled him.

He should have realized. As intimate as they were, he should have known she'd figured out he was ticklish. But he hadn't and he was paying for it now. Oh, boy, was he paying.

She was merciless and Natalie—his sweet, loving little daughter—only egged her on. By the time he finally made it back to the edge of the rock pond, Tad had laughed so hard his ribs hurt.

He shook his head at the two of them in reprimand. "See if I make my special sauce tonight. Just see. It'll be gunk out of a bottle for the two of you."

"Oh, no!" Natalie exclaimed. "You have to make it. You have to!"

Lisa gave her a puzzled look. "It's that great?"

The little girl nodded. "It's the best, the absolute best."

"Oh, well, then, if it's that good we'll have to see what we can do to convince him."

They advanced through the water as one, wiggling their fingers.

Tad gave up with as good grace as he could muster. He threw up both hands and managed a look of pure male haughtiness despite an almost-irresistible desire to grin.

"I surrender."

That sent his "girls" into hoots of laughter that continued until all three of them were out of the pond and toweled dry. Together, they walked back up to the house.

Miss Harris was having some well-deserved time off. As Lisa and Natalie went off to blow-dry their hair and do all that other girl stuff, Tad pulled a fresh pair of jeans and a shirt from the closet in his room, dressed, and padded down to the kitchen.

He'd overseen the design and construction of the house every step of the way, but the kitchen had gotten special treatment. It was macho superstar Tad Jenkins's secret that he'd considered an alternative career as a chef. He loved to cook. Give him a six-burner gas range, an array of top-of-the-line pots, a walk-in freezer and refrigerator, and a pantry that could have fed Chicago, and he was a happy man.

So complete was his absorption that he'd never allowed a single spoonful of store-bought baby food to pass his daughter's lips. He'd made his own for her, sitting her up in her high chair for taste tests and explaining to her every step of the way what he was doing.

"This is an apricot, sweetheart. You'll like it. I'm just going to add a splash of lemon juice while it's pureeing to make it more interesting.

"This is an avocado, honey. No, don't smear all of it on your face. Eat some, too. Later, we'll plant the seed.

"This is focaccia, doll face. Try out that new tooth on it."

Was it any wonder that her third word was "cook"? All right, maybe it was "coo," but close enough.

He was smiling over that when the girls joined him. Lisa had seen part of the house earlier when they arrived but she hadn't been in the kitchen before. She looked around in amazement.

Along with the great room that opened directly onto it, the kitchen took up almost half of the first floor. It was easily as large as any apartment Lisa had ever had.

White marble veined with black and gray formed the counters that gleamed above darkly polished teak cabinets. Recessed lighting illuminated the bleached-oak floors. Walls of glass brought the outside in, and further added to the sense of endless space.

In addition to the six-burner gas stove there was another, equally large, that contained a grill and deep fryer above a second oversize oven. Twin convection ovens were built into wall cabinets. There was a triple array of sinks, all white porcelain, one with a separate faucet that seemed to be for nothing other than washing vegetables.

But what struck her most was that there was no refrigerator. At first, she thought she must have missed it, probably because it was paneled over with wood to match the cabinets. But no, there really wasn't one. She looked more closely and spotted the heavy metal door standing partially open.

"Let me guess," she said, indicating it. "That's the fridge?"

"And freezer." Tad gestured to double, wooden doors nearby. "The pantry's through there."

"You could feed an army out of this place."

"Possibly, but right now I'm going to feed the three of us. First I have to ask you a really personal question."

Natalie was right there, looking from one to the other of them, missing nothing. Even so, Lisa felt just a wee bit nervous. How much more personal could they possibly get? "What?"

"How do you really feel about garlic?"

Once she'd assured him that she adored garlic, believing it the most perfect of nature's creations and an adornment to any meal, he went to work. Before long, the kitchen filled with aromas that made Lisa's mouth water. To think she'd dared to make sandwiches for this man. Undoubtedly he'd just eaten them to be polite.

By contrast, she ate every morsel of the dinner he prepared because it was the most enticingly delicious meal she'd ever had. Working in advertising, she'd had her share of overpriced restaurant food served up in absurdly pompous surroundings, but she'd never eaten anything like this. She could taste every separate ingredient even as they all melded together on her tongue in a way that sent happy little shivers right through her.

With a start, she realized that he brought the same care to preparing food that he brought to making love. He was a connoisseur in both areas, and an unabashed sensualist.

He was also darn good company. So was Natalie. Dinner passed quickly as the three of them laughed, swapped stories and generally enjoyed themselves. Too soon it was over. As was the way with children, Natalie went from being a bright flame of energy to visibly drooping, with hardly a breath in between.

"I'll clear up," Lisa said softly as Tad lifted his little daughter from her chair.

"You don't have to do that."

"I don't mind," she assured him.

Natalie opened her eyes just slightly and smiled sleepily. "Night, Lisa."

"Night, pixie," she said softly.

The kitchen was clean by the time he returned. Lisa was just putting the last plate in the dishwasher. "Is Natalie asleep?" she asked.

"Before Georgie Rabbit could find all the Easter eggs."

"Excuse me?"

He grinned. "It's her favorite story. She likes you, by the way."

"I like her, too."

"She also thinks you're beautiful."

Lisa looked surprised. "She said that?"

"Oh, yeah, right along with reminding me that I'm not getting any younger and good women are hard to come by."

"What?"

He shrugged unapologetically. "I know she's only five but she's smart as a whip. One of the reasons I protect her so much is that she picks up on everything, and I mean *everything*."

He hooked his thumbs through the belt loops of his jeans and focused somewhere over Lisa's left shoulder. "As far as Natalie knows, you're the first woman I've dated since her mother. She doesn't want me to blow it."

"I don't understand...."

"I've never let her meet any woman I've been involved with," he explained, his eyes meeting hers. "Until now."

Lisa was having trouble swallowing. First, his extraordinary gift to her the night before and now this. It was almost more than she could take in.

"Does that mean you've never brought another woman here?" she asked.

He nodded. His eyes were smoky, tantalizing her. He stepped closer, almost but not quite touching her. "Except for Miss Harris, of course."

"Of course..."

But the redoubtable Miss Harris was gone for the night, visiting friends. Except for the sleeping child, they were alone in the house.

The great room was exactly as the name implied—

two stories high from the flagstone floor to the beamed ceiling, with an immense stone fireplace at one end and a wall of glass commanding a sweeping view of the river.

Couches were set before the fireplace, lacquered tables were scattered about, and the floor was partly covered by rare Oriental rugs. The table where they had eaten dinner was set on a small rise off to one side. Fully open, it could seat twelve comfortably but it was arranged for just six now. Cabinets behind it held an array of china and books. The whole effect was luxurious without being overdone. For all its impressiveness, the room looked well enjoyed.

Tad led her over to one of the couches. She settled back against the curve of his shoulder and sighed.

"I should be going soon."

His arm tightened. He put a hand under her chin, compelling her to look at him. "Why?"

She was surprised that he had to ask. "I just presumed... I didn't think you'd want...with Natalie here...."

The corners of his mouth quirked. "Let me see if I can put that into a sentence. You presumed I wouldn't want you to stay with me here because of my daughter."

She flushed but only partly with embarrassment. She was also a little annoyed at him. Why did they have to dwell on the obvious? "I know you've broken a rule by introducing me to her at all. It just makes sense that you wouldn't want her to realize we—"

She broke off, not quite as bold as she'd thought she was, especially not when his free hand had slipped down to cup her breast, closing over it with blatant possessiveness while the hand that had held her chin was gently stroking her cheek. She was helpless to conceal her instant response. Her nipple hardened, pressing against his palm.

"That we're sharing a bed?" he murmured huskily. "It's not going to do her any harm to know that. She'll find out eventually anyway."

Lisa opened her mouth to reply, then shut it again. He was suggesting that their relationship wasn't going to be brief. Did he mean just until the end of the Teal River Project? But that was months off, if not much longer considering all the follow-up that would have to be done and...

She'd told him the truth when she said she believed him about Melanie. But she still had to face reality straight on. While there was no doubt that he enjoyed her thoroughly, it was equally true that he had known many women in his life and had shown every sign of needing variety. There was no reason to think that had changed.

The plain fact was that she would have to be a self-destructive fool to believe their relationship was anything but temporary. That she had violated the beliefs of a lifetime in order to be with him changed nothing so far as that was concerned. She would simply have to live with the aftermath, as she had always known she would.

But if that was the case, then she damn well wasn't going to waste a moment.

She eased a leg up beneath her short skirt and let her thigh rub between his. His response was instant and unmistakable.

"In that case," she murmured, nibbling on his ear, "I suggest we turn in."

Natalie seemed pleased but not at all surprised to find Lisa at the breakfast table the next morning. The little girl greeted her with a friendly smile and plopped down in the chair next to her.

In a confidential tone, she said, "If Daddy's in a really good mood, he'll make French toast. He makes the best French toast in the world."

Lisa saw no reason to doubt it, especially not when Tad emerged from the kitchen a few minutes later with a smile of his own and a platter of the most delectable looking—and smelling—French toast she'd ever encountered.

It was thicker than she was used to, softer and fluffier, with a light dusting of confectioner's sugar and cinnamon. Each perfect slice sat in a pool of warmed maple syrup—not the gooey artificial stuff but the real thing from actual trees.

"I've died," Lisa said when she had swallowed the first forkful. "And I must have led a really good life because this has to be heaven."

Tad gave her a glance that could only be described as devilish, leaned over and murmured very softly, "I swear you didn't react this enthusiastically last night."

She ducked her head, hoping Natalie wouldn't see her blush, but couldn't resist replying, "Then you must not remember it as clearly as I do." To refresh his memory, she reached over beneath the cover of the table and lightly raked her nails up the inside of his thigh.

"I stand corrected," he murmured and after that paid strict attention to breakfast.

"That's right, honey," Tad said a few hours later. "Straight into Lincoln's mouth."

"It's hard," Natalie complained. "He keeps shutting it."

The Great Emancipator—or at least a large mechanical version of him—was slowly opening and closing his hinged mouth. His stovepipe hat rose and lowered to the same rhythm, just distracting enough to make it all the harder to get the golf ball through.

"Watch the timing," Tad advised. "Tap the ball as soon as the mouth finishes closing, just before it starts opening again."

Natalie tried it and squealed with delight when it worked. She stood patiently as Tad and Lisa took their own turns, then headed on to the next hole—a large wooden Christmas tree fully decorated and festooned with lights.

The evening was warm, verging on balmy. It had brought out a good number of people to the miniature golf course beside a small lake. Others were out on the water in small boats, lazily rowing. Still more were picnicking along the shore.

"What a nice place," Lisa said quietly. She was fully aware that Tad had been recognized, but once again no one bothered them. She got far more curious stares than either he or Natalie but she was having too much fun to care.

When they finished playing, they wandered over to the funfair. All the rides were geared to younger children. Natalie scrambled from the small carousel to the bumper cars and spinning tea cups and back again.

"I'm getting dizzy watching her," Lisa admitted after a while.

"Just think how she'll sleep tonight," Tad said and patted her bottom, his hand lingering just a moment.

She started and glared at him. He gave her a look of innocent bewilderment and laughed.

Natalie was asleep on her father's shoulder when they got back to the house. Lisa helped put her to bed. She stood with Tad for a few minutes in the shadowed bedroom, their arms around each other's waists, and felt such a piercing sense of contentment that it brought tears to her eyes.

They were settling on the couch downstairs with an open bottle of wine and Vivaldi on the stereo when a key turned in the front door. Lisa stiffened but Tad merely stood, glanced toward the hall and said, "Good evening, Miss Harris."

The woman who nodded pleasantly to him in response wasn't Lisa's idea of an English nanny. For one thing, she didn't seem to be wearing anything starched; just nice, soft clothes that looked comfortable on her matter-of-factly plump form. She also had an absolutely lovely smile and warm, dancing eyes.

"Good evening, sir. I trust you and Natalie had a pleasant day?"

"Very much so, thank you." He held out a hand to Lisa, bringing her to stand beside him. "I'd like to introduce Miss Preston. She's staying with us."

For just a moment, Miss Harris looked surprised. Lisa remembered what Tad had said about never before bringing a woman to his home. She wondered what the nanny would think of it and prayed she wouldn't mind. Miss Harris was obviously far too good with Natalie, and far too important to her, to be taken lightly.

But she was also a kind and generous person who respected her employer and trusted his judgment completely. "It's nice to meet you, Miss Preston," she said with genuine courtesy.

"And you, Miss Harris, but I wish you would call me Lisa."

"In that case, you must call me Delphinia, dear."

It was Tad's turn to look surprised. When the nanny had bidden them both good-night and departed for her own quarters, he said, "Delphinia? I guess I knew that was her first name, but *I've* never been invited to use it."

"Of course not," Lisa said lightly. She was feeling very relieved now that she'd met the redoubtable Miss Harris—Delphinia—and been accepted by her. "You're 'sir.' She would never presume to such familiarity with you."

He sized that up, watching her, and smiled slowly. "You like her."

"I was all set to before I met her. Natalie's a very happy child, so obviously Delphinia is a good person."

"She's great." Having concluded that subject to his satisfaction, he drew Lisa into his arms. "So what would you like to do tonight?"

She gave him a mischievous smile. "Oh, I don't know. Any chance there's a 'Twilight Zone' marathon on? We could make popcorn and stay up all night watching."

"No such luck," he growled, his hands clasping her hips, moving her slowly against him.

"Too bad. You don't play gin rummy, do you?"

"Strictly poker." He kept up the gentle, provocative motion, smiling all the while.

"I've always wanted to learn to play poker. You could teach me."

"I could do that," he agreed as he lowered his head and gently raked his teeth down her throat. "But only if the stakes are right."

"What stakes do you want?" she asked, not quite able to keep her voice steady.

He blew lightly in her ear, making her quiver. His

voice was low and husky as he murmured, "Just you, babe. All of you, every way I want you, all night."

Her bones were melting. It was only sheer fortitude that held her upright. That and his hands hard on her hips.

"What if I win?"

He laughed. "Same deal. You get me."

Lisa grinned. She caught his face between her palms and kissed him deeply. When they broke apart finally, both were breathing hard.

"I don't see how I can lose," she said.

Half an hour later, sitting cross-legged on the huge bed in the master suite, Lisa shook her head in disgust. "I can't believe I lost, not that fast."

Tad shrugged complacently. "Poker's a complex game."

"I think you should give me another chance. After all, I'm just a learner."

He looked at the exquisite woman on his bed, her chestnut hair curling around her shoulders, her skirt hiked up to reveal stupendous legs, her translucent skin glowing, and murmured, "A fast one, I'd say."

"Come on, let's play another hand."

"Maybe, if you make it interesting."

She raised an eyebrow. "Considering the stakes, I'm not sure how that's possible."

"Easy. I'm even willing to play several more hands, but every time you lose, you have to take something off. When you're naked, the game's over and I collect my winnings.''

Her tongue eased out ever so slightly to moisten her lips. She wasn't taking her eyes off him. "Strip poker."

"A fine American pastime."

"I suppose we could...."

He dealt the cards. Play went back and forth for several minutes but all too quickly, she lost again. "Maybe I should have dressed more warmly for this," Lisa said as she slowly unbuttoned her blouse and removed it.

His gaze was more than warm all by itself. "You've got the advantage, honey. I'm not wearing anything but jeans and briefs."

With that information to encourage her, she tried again but darned if he didn't draw a pair of queens that beat anything she had. Her skirt joined the blouse. She was left in nothing but her skimpy bra and panties.

"I have to win eventually," she said.

"Absolutely."

But luck wasn't with her. He won the next hand easily. He didn't say anything, just sat back at the foot of the bed and waited. With more self-consciousness than she would have expected, all things considered, Lisa unhooked her bra. She hesitated a moment or two but finally removed it. Cool air brushed the nipples that were already peaked.

There was something surpassingly erotic about sit-

ting on the bed opposite him bare-breasted, no concealment left except for the triangle of lace between
her legs. Sooner or later that would go, too, and then
he would, as he had said, "collect."

She was undeniably excited and well aware that he
knew it. It was impossible to conceal anything from
this man who understood her body better than she did
herself.

All the same, she really did want to win at least
one hand. It wasn't to be, though. Not that night, anyway. Five minutes later, Tad tossed down his cards
and with a broad smile, said, "Finish it, sweetheart."

She stood at the side of the bed. Vividly aware that
he was watching her every movement, she slid the
panties down her legs and let them drop to the floor.

He looked at her. Really looked. His gaze went up
and down every inch of her, lingering on her breasts
and the shadowed apex of her thighs. Huskily, he
said, "Turn around."

Trying to deny the shiver of anticipation that his
words evoked was useless. Slowly, she turned. With
her back to him, it should have been easier but it
wasn't. Staring at the wall opposite the bed, she en-
dured through long moments until finally she heard
him take a deep breath. "Again."

Once more, she obeyed and faced him. His eyes
glittered, the skin drawn tautly over chiseled features.
Her own gaze drifted to the bulge in his jeans. He
was fully, heavily aroused.

"Get on the bed," he said and stood. In one swift movement, he removed his clothes.

Lisa was trembling in earnest when she lay on her back. She told herself she had absolutely nothing to be afraid of; surely he had proved that the other night. But all the same she felt so completely vulnerable, so unable to deny him anything he wished.

As though he sensed her unease, Tad stretched out beside her. For a few moments, he did nothing. Only when she stirred restlessly did he begin to caress her. He was very slow and very thorough. Before long, Lisa had forgotten all about fulfilling his demands and was making her own.

He laughed at that and kept on as he had been doing until her voice broke and she pleaded with him. Then he left no doubt at all that in this particular game there were indeed only winners.

Chapter 16

Monday morning brought a return to work and a new source of self-consciousness for Lisa. To all intents and purposes, she had moved out of the cottage. She wondered if any of her colleagues would notice and if they did, if it would affect her ability to work with them.

Either they hadn't or it didn't. The day went smoothly. She even managed to sit through another meeting that included Tad and keep her mind on business, more or less.

There was also the satisfaction of knowing that her part of the project was going very well. The ideas flowed from her with that special resonance anyone who did creative work would understand. The sense of rightness assured her she would be able to reach into the hearts and minds of the people who would call Teal River home.

That evening, she and Tad spent several pleasant hours with Natalie. When it was her bedtime, they tucked her in together, then went out to dinner. The next evening, they stayed in, sharing dinner with Natalie and Delphinia, and watching TV together.

Lisa noted that Tad checked the program schedule ahead of time, selected what Natalie could view and kept the clicker close at hand even then. He turned the set off as the promo started for another show— one clearly not suitable for young children—clicking it back on when it was over.

"It's too bad more parents aren't that conscientious," Lisa said. She knew her own siblings kept very close tabs on their children's TV viewing, but she doubted even they took as much care as Tad.

Of course, he had more than the usual reason for doing so. He was determined that his daughter wouldn't hear any of the gossip that swirled around him.

The rest of the week passed in much the same way. Lisa knew that they were falling into a routine, like a family. She cherished it even as she tried not to forget that it would end inevitably.

On Friday, as work was winding down, Miss Harris suggested that Natalie might like to come with her to visit a cousin who had a farm about a hundred miles away. They would spend the weekend and undoubtedly have a splendid time.

Natalie agreed immediately, then spent half an hour convincing her father that she would not have any problem sleeping away from home. When she ran upstairs to start packing, Tad gave the nanny a grateful look, which prompted a broad smile in return.

By sundown, he and Lisa had the house to themselves. They went to bed very early and fell asleep very late. Rising the next morning, they had a leisurely brunch.

The bright day beckoned. When Tad suggested they go riding, Lisa didn't hesitate. It helped that he assured her of a gentle mare who wouldn't tax her abilities.

They rode to the meadow where they had been before. Lisa hadn't been on a horse in years and was surprised how readily the rhythm of it returned to her. Tethering their mounts near the river, they walked hand in hand among the wildflowers.

Neither felt any need to speak. They were completely at ease with one another in the way more common to lovers of many years. Perhaps it was due to the intensity of their relationship or perhaps because of the instinctive affinity that had existed from the very beginning. Whatever the cause, there was no awkwardness or hesitation between them. They walked for a time and when they had done that enough, they sank very naturally to the flower-draped ground.

Lisa lay looking up at the sky, remembering when Tad had begun to make love to her in this same place.

Turning her head toward him, she murmured, "Why did you stop?"

He lay on his side, teasing her mouth with a blunt-tipped finger. She opened her lips and sucked his finger in, laving him with her tongue.

"It was too soon," he said, his voice thickening. "Or at least I thought it was. I didn't know..."

She bit his finger gently before releasing it. Her eyes were alight with pleasure and sheer, feminine power. "Know what?"

"How it would be between us. How well we would—"

"Fit together," she suggested.

He laughed. "Yes, that's it. Fit together. I'd say we do that quite extraordinarily well."

"You're the expert."

Although she spoke lightly enough, he frowned. Brushing her cheek with the back of his hand, he asked, "Do you mind that?"

"That you've been with other women? I can't say it thrills me, but I suppose I should appreciate all that experience since I benefit from it so greatly."

"That's very generous of you, but I wonder if it would really have been any different. We would just have learned together."

Her hand touched his face gently. "Don't regret the past. It made you the man you are, and that's nothing to be sorry about."

What she said seemed very simple to her but he clearly felt otherwise. His eyes held a sudden sheen as he gathered her close. "You're an incredible woman. A few weeks ago, I wouldn't have believed that someone like you existed."

His powerful arms were very tight around her but Lisa didn't care. She could have stayed like that forever.

In time, however, other needs arose. They began to touch, slowly and gently. Their bodies were so well attuned, and they felt no rush. Tad slipped her top over her head as she undid the buttons of his shirt. He shrugged it off as a butterfly wafted straight between them, making them both laugh.

"Get your own girl," Tad advised.

The butterfly went off, perhaps to do just that, and they stretched out together on the carpet of flowers. Their kisses were long and deep, infinitely pleasuring all by themselves. Lisa's eyes were smoky with desire when Tad reached for the front closure of her bra.

And froze...

His head went back and his nostrils actually flared. In an instant, he went from being her lover to being someone she could scarcely recognize—harsh, cold, every sense on the alert and ready for battle.

"What..." she began.

He silenced her with a hand over her mouth. "Don't move."

She obeyed simply because she had no choice. The weight of his body pressed her down into the concealing flowers. Silence drifted over them both.

She wanted to ask again what could possibly be

wrong but even after his hand eased, she didn't dare.
She could only lie there as his head turned ever so
slightly in one direction and then another.

To an observer at a distance, it would merely have
looked as though he was caressing the woman under
him. Only she realized that he was scanning the
ground all around them. She felt the steely strength
gathering in his body and was almost, if not quite
prepared, when he suddenly exploded into motion.

Frantically, she gathered her blouse back together
and began buttoning it as she sat up. Tad ran with the
speed and agility of a natural hunter. He reached the
trees at the edge of the meadow and disappeared into
them.

Moments passed. Lisa heard the sounds of a strug-
gle and then a scream. Heart pounding, she leaped to
her feet and ran after him. Tad was on his knees on
the ground. His fists were knotted around the jacket
of the man who lay beneath him, screaming frantically.

"Lemme go! You can't do this! Son of a bitch,
lemme go!"

Beside the man, lying where it had landed in the
dirt, was a camera with a telephoto lens attached.

Lisa put a hand to her mouth. A horrible, crawling
sensation overtook her. She cried out.

Tad looked up, saw her, and rasped an order. "Get
away from here!"

He looked furious, in the grip of such rage that she
actually feared for him. Hard on that came the reali-

zation that she should really fear for the man he had caught.

Instead of leaving, she came closer. The man was middle-aged, stocky and balding. His face was red with his exertions and streaked with dirt.

"Who is he?" she asked.

"He's a damn paparazzi. Who do you think he is? He was taking pictures of us."

Her stomach churned. She'd known the instant she saw the camera, but to hear it confirmed—

"I mean, do you know him, have you seen him before?"

Tad bared his teeth in what couldn't possibly be mistaken for a smile. "Oh, yeah, I know him. Sammy Blair, best in the business. Got the topless shots of Princess Di and a few other real winners along the those lines. Seems like he was going for the same thing today."

He shook the man hard, sending his head lolling back and forth. "That was it, wasn't it, Sammy? Looking to peddle a little flesh, were you? I'm going to guess it was you in L.A."

Despite the awkwardness of his position, at least some of the photographer's bravado seemed to be returning. Maybe the nature of his occupation made such encounters not entirely unexpected.

"Good guess, Jenkins. Only I got Melanie in the altogether, not just on top. She didn't mind. Hell, she set it up. Too bad you're not as cooperative. If you'd kept on a little longer, I could've retired on the proceeds.''

If he kept talking like that much longer, Lisa decided, she was going to demand her own turn with him. Instead, she picked up the camera. Blair saw what she was about to do and yelled.

"Hey, put that down. You can't..."

She could and she did. The roll of film sprang free and unraveled. She held it all out to the light, letting every image on it dissolve into nothingness.

When she was done, she threw the camera back down, not caring if it shattered. "You're disgusting, a parasite. If I ever see you again, you won't have to worry about Tad. I'll go after you myself."

Blair stared at her for a moment. Slowly, his small eyes crinkled. "A feisty one. No wonder you were so hot for her, Jenkins. Who is she?"

"You've got no goddamn sense at all, do you?" Tad growled. He stood, dragging the photographer upright. With one hand at the nape of his neck and the other on the seat of his pants, he pushed Blair forward. "Where's your car?"

"About half a mile from here. Hey, c'mon, we can cut a deal. You don't want any nudies, okay by me. Just let me get something nice with the two of you. Holding hands, even. Anything. Jeez, you walked away from Melanie George *and* a hundred-million-dollar deal. People want to know why."

"Go to hell," Tad said. He was calmer now but not all that much. Abruptly, he let go of Blair and shoved him forward, so hard that the photographer went down on his knees in the dirt.

"I'm giving you a fifteen-minute head start," Tad said as the other man struggled back up to his feet. "If you're not gone by then, you'd better pray your health insurance is as good as you think."

"You can't hit me," Blair retorted, angrily dusting himself off. "I've got rights. I'll sue—"

"You're on my land," Tad stated. "And you upset my woman. That's all the right I need." He leaned down close so that he and Blair were eye-to-eye. In a voice that sent chills down Lisa's spine, he said, "This is the last chance you get. *Run.*"

Blair ran. He didn't do it particularly well or fast, but he was energetic about it. He looked back over his shoulder once. Whatever he saw in Tad's face spurred him to go even faster. Within moments, he had disappeared.

Lisa let her breath out slowly. She felt vaguely nauseous from the encounter yet undeniably excited, even triumphant. Blair had tried and failed. They had won.

Now, if only she could get Tad to see it that way.

Tad did calm down eventually but it took a while, and he absolutely refused to see what Lisa thought was the humor of the situation.

"You don't think it was funny how he had the gall to try to make a deal with you when you were that far away from choking him?" She held up her thumb and index finger with almost no space between them.

"C'mon, you've got to give him a little credit for that."

Tad grumbled, disgusted. They were in the kitchen. He was cooking. It seemed to make him feel better. "What I should have given him was my fist in both eyes. Maybe if they were sealed closed for a while, he'd reconsider life as a Peeping Tom."

Lisa realized his anger wasn't for himself. He'd only apologized to her about a dozen times, telling her how sorry he was that it had happened. She had to point out over and over that not all that much *had* happened. They'd been caught kissing and she'd had her blouse off but with her bra still in place. She'd been at least as well covered as she would have been at the beach.

That brought him up short. "What do you mean?" he demanded. "That bra's pretty skimpy. You don't wear stuff like that at the beach."

"I wear bikinis," she said and took a sip of the wine he'd poured for her. "Why should that surprise you? Plenty of women do."

"Not women who—" He stopped, seemingly at a loss for words.

"Who what?"

"Who are virgins like you were and who look like you."

"Oh, you're an expert on this, too? Since when did you learn so much about the fashion preferences of virgins?"

"Since never. Don't try to change the subject. I

don't want you parading around any beach in a bikini. You'll cover up more than that.''

"What do you expect me to wear, a shroud?''

"Of course not. A nice, sensible one-piece will be fine. And not one of those with the leg holes cut up to the waist. Something more...demure than that.''

Lisa started to choke. This man who had turned her into a creature of pure sensuality wanted her how? "Demure? You want me to look demure?''

"In public, damn straight I do. I don't want men seeing you and wondering what it would be like to have you in bed.''

"Men do that? Men seriously look at a woman they don't even know and imagine...?''

"Yeah,'' he said with an unabashed grin. "We do. You've got to face it, sugar, we're just your basic grunt-and-scratch mammal. See something we want, we go straight for it. Libido rules.''

"I don't believe that. Men are every bit as capable of higher thought as women. Why, men write symphonies and paint beautiful pictures and...'' She gestured at him. "And even cook divinely. You can't just always be thinking about...''

"Having sex,'' he supplied helpfully.

Her face tightened. Not looking at him, she said, "I was going to say 'making love,' but I guess that would sound stupid.''

He sighed and put down the whisk he'd been using. She was in his arms a moment later. Lisa stiffened and tried to push him away, but truth be told, it was a halfhearted effort. She had no resistance at all where he was concerned, and hadn't she already proved it time after time?

"'Making love' does sound a lot better," he admitted softly. "At least where we're concerned."

He was doing it again. She was hungry, dammit. She wanted to eat. But was she? Oh, no, not for a while at least. She was going to let him lead her right up the stairs to the bedroom and—

"Let's do it on the floor," he said and pulled her down on top of him.

He was more cheerful after that and he did—finally—feed her. But she could sense that he was on edge throughout the remainder of the weekend. By Sunday evening, she was glad that Natalie was home to distract him.

Monday, Lisa headed over to her office to get to work. Tad planned to spend the day catching up with the accountants and lawyers by conference call and E-mail. He would be working at the house.

She grabbed a cup of coffee in the common room, flipped on her computer and started in right away at the keyboard, getting down all the thoughts that had come to her over the weekend. A soft smile lit her eyes as she considered how incredibly productive she'd become despite the huge distraction of loving Tad.

It was scary to even think that word but she'd started doing it, if only in her own mind. She wasn't about to say anything to him. She still felt so over-whelmed where he was concerned, so fragile and vul-nerable, that she couldn't bear to expose anything more of herself.

In the years she'd worked in advertising, she'd be-come accustomed to planning out everything well in advance. It wasn't unusual for her to be working on a campaign six months or even a year before it would reach the public. She couldn't count the number of times she'd written the next instead of the current year on checks or correspondence because she was so at-tuned to the future.

But not now. Now she existed only in the present, even the moment. She refused to think about what was going to happen between her and Tad. They came from such entirely different worlds and their lives had taken such different courses, it was remarkable that they could come together at all. Beyond that, she would be foolish to ask for anything.

Yet there were times, despite her best resolve, when she caught her thoughts drifting in that direc-tion. When they were together in the aftermath of making love and he held her so tenderly; when they were with Natalie being a family together; even when she was alone and her heart overruled her mind.

Enough of that now. If she needed a break from work—and after so many hours, she was willing to admit that she did—she would make it a lot more useful than woolgathering. There were several things she needed from town.

She would drive in, do a little shopping, maybe see if she could find something Natalie would like. The little girl had the usual trove of toys one would expect for a child with a doting father, but she wasn't at all spoiled. She was just as happy making a birdhouse out of a milk container as she was playing with anything more elaborate.

Wondering what Tad—and Delphinia—would say to finger paint, Lisa grabbed her bag and headed for the car. Until she was actually on her way, she didn't realize that this was the first time she'd done anything alone in days—apart from just work.

That had to be a record for her. She'd always been a private person. Frequent periods of solitude had been as necessary to her as food and rest. Lately, she'd known nothing of the sort. Even her body no longer seemed entirely her own, so perfectly attuned had it become to Tad's touch.

A couple of hours alone should have been welcome but as she drove toward town, Lisa caught herself feeling impatient to finish her errands and get back. The plain fact was that solitude no longer had much appeal for her. If she was going to be alone, she would much rather do it with Tad.

She found a parking spot along the single street, got out and headed for the drugstore she'd noticed before. She needed the usual things—shampoo, conditioner and so on.

A display of nutritional supplements caught her eye as she was waiting to pay. Invariably healthy and addicted to a good diet, she hadn't taken a vitamin since she was a kid and hadn't paid all that much attention to the various health crazes that swept the country from time to time. Now she was amused to note the promises being made—restore youth and vitality... build muscle mass...increase sexual potency.

Now, there was a thought. Her mouth twitched as she considered the effects of any increase in sexual potency on Tad's part. She had a feeling they were setting some sort of record as it was. Any more, and...

Her gaze drifted to the rack of newspapers in front of the cash registers. There were the usual assortment, mostly at least semilegitimate, with the tabloids thrown in for color. One of the latter featured a photograph that took up most of the front page, offset only by the blaring headline:

Tad Jenkins In Lovenest With Mystery Woman

Lisa's throat closed. She couldn't swallow, couldn't breathe, couldn't make a sound. Helpless, she stared at the photo of herself and Tad lying in the meadow.

It was remarkably clear, given the distance from which it must have been taken. What was it Tad had said about the paparazzi having better equipment than the CIA? Anyone could clearly see that his finger was in her mouth and that she was enjoying it.

Her stomach twisted. For a horrible moment, she thought she was going to be sick right there on the floor of the drugstore.

It passed, but only barely, and it threatened to return when she saw the line of type at the bottom of the photo:

More Pics Inside!

Her hand was shaking so badly that she could barely control it but she managed to pick up a copy of the tabloid. She even managed to pay for it along with her other purchases, walk out of the store and get back to her car before her legs gave way entirely.

For several minutes, she couldn't do anything except grip the steering wheel and take deep breaths. She didn't touch the paper again, didn't even consider looking inside it. Concentrating strictly on driving, she returned to Teal River.

Tad was waiting in her office. He unfolded his long body from the chair next to her desk and stood as she entered. One look at her face told him everything. He didn't even need to see the paper sticking out of the top of the bag she carried.

"You know," he said.

She nodded and set the bag down. "I went into town to get a few things and saw it." She'd had time to think in the car, time to gain some perspective.

Yes, she felt horribly exposed and violated, but she was too honest to exaggerate that. Plenty of other people had been through far worse than having a few unwanted photos of themselves published in a scandal sheet. She wasn't going to let this get out of hand.

"Sammy must be more clever than we thought," she said and was very pleased by how calm she sounded.

Tad stared at her. His hands were jammed deep in the pockets of his jeans. He hadn't bothered tying his hair back; it fell, dark and wild, to his massive shoulders. His eyes glittered harshly. He looked dangerous, untamed, utterly male.

Warmth pooled in her belly. She could think of a lot of things she would rather be doing with him just then instead of talking about a few photos.

"It was my fault," he said tautly. "I should have realized he'd been in the business too long not to take precautions. He must have shot a few photos for insurance, pocketed that roll and loaded the one we took. It's been done before."

"What's done is done."

Ordinarily, she would have ripped her tongue out before resorting to such a cliché. But her brain wasn't working all that well at the moment. She was still far more disturbed by the photos than she was willing to let on to Tad. And she was finding a whole different sort of disturbance being close to him.

"I can't believe you're so relaxed about this," he said. Yanking the tabloid out of the bag, he dropped it on her desk and stared at the front page. "One of my lawyers called this morning to make sure I knew about it.''

"Nice of him," Lisa replied sarcastically. What was it that compelled people to want to deliver bad news?

"He was just doing his job. This is liable to unleash a whole lot more of the same."

Her composure cracked. "What do you mean?" she asked shakily.

"Sammy's hardly the only paparazzi out there. Now that the rest know there's meat to be had, they'll be going after it, too."

Her stomach was back to clenching. It hadn't occurred to her that this could be anything but an isolated incident. "Teal River is private property. Surely you can keep them away."

"I can try," he agreed. "But it won't do much good unless they're caught trespassing. Besides, with the equipment they've got, we won't be able to go anywhere near the boundaries—much less into town—without being fair game."

Without waiting for her response, he flipped the paper open and looked at the pictures inside. Lisa peeked at them over his shoulder. They weren't as bad as the one on the front—just photos of her and Tad walking across the field, talking, sinking down amid the flowers, kissing.

She really wasn't going to be sick. Or if she was, she was damn well going to do it in the ladies' room.

"Excuse me," she said and walked out hurriedly.

When she came back a few minutes later, she felt better. A little shaky still, but better. Sometimes you just had to let nature take its course.

Tad was using the phone on her desk. He hung up as she came in and looked at her narrowly. "You okay?"

"Fine." With the best smile she could muster, she said, "You know that one on the cover is really a lot better than my high-school yearbook picture, not to mention what's in my passport."

He ignored the rather pitiful attempt at humor and came around to the other side of the desk. Taking hold of her shoulders, he asked, "Have you thought about how your family is going to react?"

She hadn't, not until then, and she certainly didn't want to, but he was forcing her to confront it.

"They don't buy these things," she said.

"And they don't shop anywhere they're sold or know anyone who does read them?" His face tightened, becoming hard and unyielding. "You honestly think they're not going to find out?"

"It doesn't matter. They're intelligent people, kind and caring. They won't jump to any conclusions."

"I wouldn't expect them to be anything less, being your parents. But they'll think exactly what these photos are supposed to make anyone think—that we're lovers. How's that going to make them feel?"

Before she could reply, he drew her closer to him, cupping the nape of her neck in one big hand as the other pressed against the small of her back.

"I'm a parent myself," he reminded her. "I know how I'd feel if my daughter was involved with a man with a reputation for treating women like fast food."

She couldn't help it; the comparison struck her as funny. Given his culinary predilections, she realized he meant it as a grave insult. She just couldn't take it that way.

"Now wait a second. There's nothing wrong with the occasional cheeseburger and fries, and those chicken nuggets..."

"You know perfectly well what I mean," he said sternly. "Ever since I got old enough to figure out what girls were for, I've seen them as a convenience, nothing more. I've never allowed myself to get emotionally involved, until now. Women were strictly interchangeable, good for just one purpose and—"

Lisa stiffened. She pressed her hands against his chest—hard. "Whoa, back up. What was that 'until now' part?"

He hesitated. For just a moment, she had the startling impression that he was actually feeling shy. It was gone as quickly as it had come, but it left her smiling.

"You must know I feel differently about you," he insisted, almost sulkily as though daring her to deny it.

"No," she insisted. "I don't." Just for good measure—and because she was suddenly feeling very bold—she added, "How could I know? I have nothing to compare you to. Maybe that's the problem.

Maybe I ought to go out, meet a few more guys, see what they're like. Then..."

His hands closed on her upper arms. He shook her lightly. "That's not funny. You're mine and if you think I'd ever let anyone else touch you—"

He broke off, finally noticing her beaming smile, and shook his head ruefully. "I sound like some kind of Neanderthal. You woman, me man, you come."

Lisa swayed closer to him, moving her hips exactly the way she knew he liked so much. A heady sense of giddiness was filling her. The "until now" part had Roman candles coming out of it.

"Sounds good to me," she said.

The dark flush that stained his cheeks told her he agreed. But he still wasn't having any of it. "Oh, no," he said firmly, and even pushed her a little distance away, although he didn't let go of her. "We're not doing that right now. And we're for sure not doing it here in your office. We're going to talk."

"Talk?"

"Talk," he confirmed grimly and set her down in the desk chair. She watched as he paced back and forth across the small area. Finally, he turned and looked at her.

"This problem with the paparazzi is just going to get worse."

Lisa nodded calmly even though she felt anything but. "I know. We'll find a way to deal with it."

"Your parents are going to be upset."

"I'll reassure them. They trust me."

"It's not good enough. You have no idea what this can do to your life. You'll feel like a captive with no freedom and no privacy. You won't want to do anything but hide."

She had to admit that when he put it that way, it sounded singularly unpleasant. But she didn't see what they could do. Unless he was thinking that she should leave....

That possibility horrified her far more than the photos had. Never mind that she'd told herself from the beginning that her time with him was only temporary. She wasn't about to let Sammy Blair or anyone else end it for them.

Jumping up, she stormed across the office and planted herself squarely in front of him.

"Now just a minute! If you think I can't handle a little pressure, you don't know me at all. I'm not about to hide from anything, and I'm especially not about to let some piece of pond scum like Sammy Blair wreck things for us. Dammit, I love you, Tad Jenkins, and if I have to, I'll shout it from the rooftops. I'll meet Sammy Scum and the rest of them head-on. They'll be so sick of seeing me, they'll run in the opposite direction. Don't you dare argue with me. I swear I'll—"

She was crying and cursing all at the same time. It was hard to do either, considering how he was kissing her. Of course, he was managing to laugh while he did it, which was no mean feat all by itself.

They clung together through long, tumultuous

minutes. When the worst of the storm had passed, Lisa found herself nestled in Tad's arms. He was sitting in the desk chair; she was in his lap.

He wiped away the last of her tears and looked down at her very seriously. "Thank you for loving me. I love you, too."

She hiccuped. "Do you really?"

His smile made her toes curl. "Oh, yeah, I really do." He said it on a note of wonder, as though marveling at the gift fate had given him.

"And," he added, "I've figured out how to handle Sammy Scum and your parents."

"How?"

He took a deep breath, tightened his arms around her and said, "When was the last time the tabloids ran photos of a boring old married couple?"

Chapter 17

Married?

Lisa gulped for air but had trouble getting any. He was looking at her very solemnly as befitted the great occasion but there was a suspicion of humor in his eyes. He knew he'd taken her by surprise and he was enjoying it, damn the man.

Married.

As in "until death do us part"? As in "happily ever after"? As in having the right to be with him every day—and every night—for the rest of her life?

Married!

Well, sure, why not?

She reached out, opened two buttons on his shirt, slid her hand inside and stroked a hard, flat nipple. "I don't know about the boring part. Do you think we can manage that?"

"No," he growled, covering her hand with his own to still her. "We'll have to fake it."

"For how long?"

"Fifty years, a hundred, as long as it takes." Her hand wouldn't be stilled. His breath was suddenly harsh. "Is there a lock on that door?"

"Don't think so."

He stood, set her back in the chair, and with a single, hard push rammed the desk up against the door, effectively barricading it.

"That takes care of that," he said, and reached for her.

"You know," Lisa said, some time later, "the foam tiles on these floors are surprisingly comfortable."

Tad laughed, a deep rumbling sound. "Remind me to thank the decorator."

He flattened his hands on either side of her and pushed himself up far enough to look into her eyes. What he saw there made him smile very tenderly. "May I assume you've accepted my proposal?"

She pretended to think about it but that didn't get very far. He did, after all, know exactly where she was most ticklish.

Bent over, rolling on the floor, hugging her middle in a vain effort to protect herself, Miss Lisa Preston agreed to become Mrs. Tad Jenkins.

Mr. Tad Jenkins was very pleased. They were delayed somewhat in leaving the office while he showed her exactly how much.

And delayed further when Lisa, in the midst of trying to reorder her clothes, said, "I can't find my panties."

Tad shrugged. He tucked his shirt into the waistband of his jeans and zipped up his fly, all the while watching her. She was wearing one of those short skirts he liked so much. The thought of her being naked underneath made him hesitate before moving the desk.

"They have to be here somewhere," he said.

She grinned, marveling that this incredible man was actually hers, as she was his. Who cared about the panties?

Two weeks before, she could not have conceived of walking out of her office in that condition. Now she wouldn't have hesitated. But Tad was having none of it. Never mind that her skirt concealed everything. He wasn't taking any chance that they would encounter someone.

At his insistence, they scrambled around until the panties were finally located in a far corner behind the credenza. Tad refused to hand them over, but held them for Lisa to step into. He drew them up her slowly, over her calves and thighs, inch by inch until they were finally back where they belonged. Straightening, he patted her behind in a decidedly proprietary fashion.

"We can go now," he said, and laughed at her glare.

Three days later, Lisa was ready to do a whole lot worse than just glare at him. She was a nervous wreck. Everything she'd ever heard about planning a wedding was turning out to be true, unfortunately.

And they weren't even having anything big. Both had agreed to a quiet ceremony and a small reception. Great, perfect, wonderful.

Nightmarish.

There was the dress, the flowers, the music, the catering, the minister, the rings—oh, right, Tad was taking care of *that* part—the invitations, the...

She couldn't think about it anymore. The top of her head would come off if she didn't stop. People got married all the time. Why did it have to be so horribly complicated?

Delphinia was helping, bless her heart. She was an island of calm in the midst of a typhoon. Natalie was wonderful. She was so happy she could barely sit down and spent every available moment hugging Tad and Lisa. At least that part was working out.

Lisa's parents were startled when she told them but undoubtedly more relieved than they wanted to let on. They trusted her judgment implicitly, just as she'd promised, and they were looking forward to meeting Tad when they arrived the next day.

Along with her brothers, their wives and children, and the dozen-or-so of Tad's friends and show-business buddies he felt close enough to include. And, oh, yes, their wives and girlfriends. Not to mention the entire staff at Teal River.

Small. Simple. No problem.

Actually, there wouldn't have been—under anything approaching normal circumstances. She'd arranged promotion campaigns that were vastly more complicated without ever breaking into a sweat. But this was different and not just because it was a wedding.

Tad wouldn't touch her.

He'd dropped that little bombshell about thirty seconds after he'd slipped a sinfully large marquis-cut diamond on her left hand. No "anything" until the wedding night. He wanted to wait.

It would have been funny except it wasn't. She knew he meant well; she was even touched by it. She just wanted to kill him.

He was sleeping in the guest room. She was tempted to nail the door shut and not let him out until the ceremony. It would make her feel better—if only a little—and it would serve him right.

Damn the man.

He knew, he absolutely knew, how much she adored what he made her feel. Her body had gotten used to being pleasured to the point of ecstasy on an extremely regular basis. She was addicted to it and she wasn't finding even a temporary return to celibacy at all pleasant.

Worse yet, she had to wonder how he could be so

calm about it. Didn't he feel what she did? Didn't he want her as much as she did him?

With such cheerful thoughts for company, Lisa got through the afternoon. About the only positive aspect of the whole situation was that there had been no further sign of Sammy Scum and his brethren.

Tad was keeping an extremely tight lid on their wedding plans. He'd also brought in what amounted to an army of private security guards, posting them all around the perimeter of Teal River with strict orders to keep all unauthorized visitors out.

For the moment at least, they were living in what amounted to an armed camp. That the local law officials had given their blessing didn't make Lisa feel a whole lot better about them. She had all sorts of reasons for wanting them to be "boring," and wanting it fast.

Two more days.

Two more long, frustrating days. And nights.

She was going to be a nervous wreck before this was over. She would probably race down the aisle, tear through her vows and attack him right there in front of everyone. At the very least, she would never get through the reception.

He wasn't going to make it. God knew, he was trying but he'd never realized before exactly how long—how very, very long—five days were.

He must have been crazy to ever come up with

such a cockamamy idea. Wait until after the ceremony? Oh, sure, piece of cake, no problem.

If he could have found a way to kick himself, he would have done it gladly.

Tad sighed. He sat back in the big chair behind the marble worktable and stared out the window. He was getting married in two days to the woman he loved more than life itself. The woman who had made him open his heart and his soul to a future he would otherwise never have known. He was going to be a husband and in time, he hoped, a father again. He was deeply, profoundly grateful.

He was going nuts.

With a groan, he got up and stretched, hoping to ease some of the tension. It didn't help. Nothing helped. He was trying to stay away from Lisa as much as possible, but every glimpse he caught—and inevitably there were many—made things worse.

He'd meant to wait because it seemed—he all but flinched at the word—romantic. She deserved that— all the hearts and flowers, violins playing, all the gooey stuff he imagined women favored. She'd been a virgin, for God's sake, and he'd never given her so much as a chance to catch her breath.

So he was doing that now, proving to himself once and for all just how bad he was at this romance stuff. Lust he had down pat, and love he was coming to terms with surprisingly fast. But romance…

Romance was torture.

Once this was over, he was never going to be romantic again. She would have to settle for hot passion and deep tenderness, with maybe a few laughs thrown in.

Two more days.

Two more nights.

He looked at his watch. It was late afternoon. They were having a noon wedding. Forty-three hours to go.

He leaned his head against the wall. Right then, the realization hit him. All he'd been thinking about was the actual wedding ceremony. He hadn't taken the reception into account.

Oh, God.

Tad didn't show up for dinner. He had some excuse—getting together with friends, something along those lines. Lisa was relieved. She'd decided she didn't want to see him while his maddening ''Don't Touch'' policy remained in effect.

She ate with Natalie and Delphinia. Despite everything, she had a fine time. With Tad away, they pigged out on microwaved hot dogs, frozen broccoli, potato chips and packaged chocolate-chip cookies. Natalie was shocked by the decadence of it all but managed to do her part. Lisa figured Delphinia had thrown in the broccoli as a sop to the child's conscience, and it worked.

It wasn't yet dark when Lisa decided to turn in. She was more tired than she wanted to admit. Who knew caterers could be so tough? Puff pastry or phyllo...grilled salmon or poached...mushroom sauce or wine...fillet or prime rib...mocha filling or...? She'd been tempted to suggest take-out but she didn't want Tad to be disappointed. Of course, she didn't want him hanging around for the meal, either.

And then there was the music. "Anything you want," he'd said. Oh, sure, let him hear one soprano belting out a high C and he would freak. People were coming who knew music—maybe not the kind she liked best, but they knew all the same. She didn't want them to be disappointed, either.

It would be all right. Everything would work out fine. She would get through this. No wonder they made it "until death do us part." You had to be screaming nuts to do this twice.

She took a shower. She got into bed. She propped the pillows up behind her and tried to read. She seemed to have forgotten how.

There was some mercy after all. In time, she slept.

Tad let himself into the house quietly. It was almost dawn. He'd deliberately stayed away as long as he could. He glanced at his watch. Thirty hours. Plus the reception.

Lisa had really worked hard on that. It wouldn't be fair to make her miss it. They would have to put in an appearance. Worse yet, two or three minutes probably wouldn't be considered enough.

The guest room was dark. He used the shower, toweled off, and got into bed naked. He was exhausted and although he absolutely never drank to excess, he'd had just a bit more than was customary for him when he drank at all. His good buddies had seen to that. If he wouldn't allow anything resembling a bachelor party—and he wouldn't—they could at least hoist a few.

The last thing Tad did before falling asleep was glance at the bedside clock—again.

Lisa woke up shortly before dawn. She didn't know what had awakened her. She was still tired, exhausted really, and she needed to sleep.

But awake she was, and too alert to hope that would change anytime soon. With a sigh, she got out of bed, put on a robe, and left the room.

She had no idea if Tad was home or not, and she wasn't going to think about that, either way. She would just check on Natalie and maybe get some milk from downstairs. If that didn't help, she would hit herself over the head with a club and be done with it.

Natalie was sleeping soundly, wrapped around her favorite stuffed animals. A wise-eyed bear watched Lisa as she tucked the covers in a little more securely and dropped a soft kiss on the child's head.

She shut the bedroom door quietly behind her and went on down the hall to the stairs. She had almost reached them when a sound from the guest room drew her up short.

She stopped, listening. It must have been her imag-

ination but for just a second she could have sworn
she heard a...

Giggle.

The faint but unmistakable sound of a woman's
giggle.

Coming from the guest room.

The room Tad had been using ever since he'd decided he wasn't going to touch *her.*

Lisa didn't hesitate, didn't think, didn't so much as
inhale. She marched straight to the door, pushed it
open, letting the light from the hallway flow into the
darkened room.

In the next instant, she wished she hadn't.

Melanie George was every bit as beautiful as her
photos indicated. And every bit as naked.

She was also in bed with Tad, sprawled on top of
him, her hand reaching to...

Lisa screamed. She opened her mouth and let out
a shout of pure rage. Melanie froze. She turned her
head, her blond hair in glorious disarray, her full lips
parted and wet, her wide eyes glazed, and stared at
Lisa.

"Who...?" she murmured.

"Wh-what?" Tad said. He sat up groggily, still
only half-awake. He, too, was naked.

Lisa took several more steps into the room. She
was shaking all over. Her hands were clenched into
fists. A red mist floated before her eyes.

Tad saw her. At the same moment, he realized they
weren't alone. He spared Melanie one horrified

glance. All the color drained from his face. "Oh, my God." He looked sick.

Lisa didn't wait. She didn't want to hear anything, and what she had to say was absolutely minimal. Seizing Melanie by the arm, she dragged her off the bed and shoved her up none too gently against the wall. A tiny pile of fabric lay on the floor. Lisa grabbed it and threw it at the blonde.

"Spray this back on," she ordered. "And while you're at it, tell me how you got in here."

"I...I...I..." Melanie was not known for her articulateness.

"How?" Lisa roared. She advanced a threatening step.

"Caterers," Melanie gasped. Being a creature of pure instinct, she had no trouble recognizing a real threat. Quickly, she wiggled into what was supposed to be a dress. "Hid in the truck... Waited..."

"Why?"

Melanie glanced at Tad. He hadn't moved but was staring at Lisa.

"Why do you think?" the actress asked, not unpleasantly. "He's the best I've ever had. I'm not going to let some little nobody steal him."

"He told you it was over."

Melanie shrugged her still-bare shoulders. Did she own any clothes at all that actually covered her? What did she do in winter? Stayed in bed, probably. Plenty for her to do there.

"Now, I'm telling you," Lisa said. She took hold

of Melanie again and dragged her toward the door. A sound from outside caught her attention. She smiled.

God bless garbagemen. One and all, they adhered to the rule that garbage had to be picked up at dawn. Amazing how they did that.

"The caterers aren't here," Lisa told Melanie. "But that's okay. You can go out with the rest of the trash."

She gave her a nice hard shove into the arms of a sweaty sanitation engineer. He looked surprised, but not displeased. Those guys were used to finding anything.

"And don't even think about trying to recycle yourself," Lisa yelled as Melanie was boosted up into the truck. "If I ever see you near *my husband* again, you won't be good for anything except parts."

The truck disappeared into the fading night. Lisa brushed her hands off and turned around. Tad was standing in front of the house, the sheet tied loosely around his lean waist, his arms folded over his broad chest, watching her.

The sight of him reminded her of just how tense she'd been feeling lately, and why. "You need to speak to those security people," she snapped. "They screwed up."

"I'll do that," he replied quietly. A moment passed. They stared at each other. Finally, he said, "You handled that really well. I've never seen Melanie take anyone so seriously."

"She called me a little nobody," Lisa said. "No way she gets away with that."

She walked up to him, tilted her head back so she could look him right in the eye, and said, "I had a big problem believing that you really wanted me instead of the string of gorgeous women you've had. But you know something? I'm over that. You'd better have meant every word you said to me—love, commitment, the whole nine yards—because you are good and stuck with me. If Melanie thinks I was rough on her, God help the next woman who tries to come near you."

He arched an eyebrow. "Is that a fact? You know, I had a problem, too. I didn't have any idea how to court a woman like you. I've thought the only thing I had going was sex so I used it all the way. But lately, I've been trying to be romantic. Somehow, I don't think it's worked."

Her eyes widened. Understanding dawned. She stared at him in disbelief. "Romantic? That's what this has been about?"

When he nodded sheepishly, she gave a shout of laughter. Giddy happiness flowed through her. He was a fantastic man—passionate, strong, tender, intelligent, funny. She absolutely adored him.

But oh, boy, did he need to get a thing or two straight. Her hands fastened on the sheet he was sort of wearing.

"I'll hold this," she said. "You hold me."

He did and very nicely, too. Her body moved

against his. Standing on her toes, she licked his earlobe just the way she knew he liked, making him tremble before she whispered softly, "Next time you're feeling romantic...?"

"Yes?" he said hoarsely.

"Try flowers."

He did. Hundreds of velvet-soft petals—roses, daisies, irises, jonquils, poppies—were sprinkled over their bridal bed. The same bed to which Mr. and Mrs. Tad Jenkins retired a short time—all right, a *very* short time—after their wedding ceremony.

*   *   *   *   *

Share in the joy of yuletide romance with brand-new
stories by two of the genre's most beloved writers

DIANA PALMER

and

JOAN JOHNSTON

in

LONE STAR CHRISTMAS

Diana Palmer and Joan Johnston share their favorite
Christmas anecdotes and personal stories in this
special hardbound edition.

Diana Palmer delivers an irresistible spin-off of her
LONG, TALL TEXANS series and Joan Johnston crafts an
unforgettable new chapter to **HAWK'S WAY** in this wonderful
keepsake edition celebrating the holiday season. So
perfect for gift giving, you'll want one for yourself...and
one to give to a special friend!

Available in November at your favorite retail outlet!

Only from

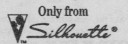

Take 4 bestselling love stories FREE

Plus get a FREE surprise gift!

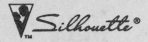

Bestselling author

JOAN JOHNSTON

continues her wildly popular miniseries with an
all-new, longer-length novel

The Virgin Groom
HAWK'S WAY

One minute, Mac Macready was a living legend in
Texas—every kid's idol, every man's envy, every
woman's fantasy. The next, his fiancée dumped him,
his career was hanging in the balance and his future
was looking mighty uncertain. Then there was the
matter of his scandalous secret, which didn't stand a
chance of staying a secret. So would he succumb to
Jewel Whitelaw's shocking proposal—or take cold
showers for the rest of the long, hot summer...?

Available August 1997
wherever Silhouette books are sold.

MATERNITY ROW

the street where little miracles are born!

The exciting new miniseries by

Paula Detmer Riggs

continues in September 1997 with

BABY BY DESIGN
(Intimate Moments #806)

Morgan Paxton returned home to find Raine, his estranged wife, pregnant with twins—after a trip to the sperm bank! Although he hadn't been the best of husbands, they were still married, and even if they didn't share his blood, these were *his* children. He wouldn't give up Raine without a fight, not when he had finally realized how much he loved her.

INTIMATE MOMENTS®
™ Silhouette®

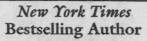

National Bestselling Author

MARY LYNN BAXTER

"Ms. Baxter's writing...strikes every chord within the female spirit."
—Sandra Brown

LONE STAR *Heat*

SHE is Juliana Reed, a prominent broadcast journalist whose television show is about to be syndicated. Until the murder...

HE is Gates O'Brien, a high-ranking member of the Texas Rangers, determined to forget about his ex-wife. He's onto something bad....

Juliana and Gates are ex-spouses, unwillingly involved in an explosive circle of political corruption, blackmail and murder.

In order to survive, they must overcome the pain of the past...and the very demons that drove them apart.

Available in September 1997 at your favorite retail outlet.

MIRA The brightest star in women's fiction   MMLBLSH